Rick and Ernie found the perfect apart... West Side. Before they're settled, Rick begins having all-too-real disturbing "dreams." Each time, an emaciated young man with sad brown eyes appears, terrifying and obsessing him.

From their next-door neighbor, Paula, Rick learns about Karl and Tommy, who lived there before them. Tommy's mysterious disappearance pains her. When she shares a photo of her with Tommy and Karl, Rick is shocked and troubled. Tommy is the man who appears to him in his dreams.

The ghostly visitations compel Rick to uncover the truth about Tommy's disappearance. It's a quest that will lead him to Karl, Tommy's lover, who may know more about Tommy's disappearance than he's telling, and a confrontation with a restless spirit who wants only to—finally—rest in peace.

WOUNDED AIR

Rick R. Reed

A NineStar Press Publication

www.ninestarpress.com

Wounded Air

Printed in the USA

ISBN: 978-1-64890-277-2

First Edition, May, 2021

Also available in eBook, ISBN: 978-1-64890-276-5

CONTENT WARNING:
This book contains sexual content, which may only be suitable for mature readers. Graphic depiction of IV drug abuse and drug addiction.

For all those who struggle in recovery and know that hope lives on the other side.

"The past never leaves us; there's always atmosphere to consider; you can wound air as cleanly as you can wound flesh. In this way, the Dream House was a haunted house. You were the sudden, inadvertent occupant of a place where bad things had happened."

—Carmen Maria Machado, *In the Dream House: A Memoir*

Before: Missing Person

Chicago Police Seek Missing 27-year-old
Ravenswood Man
By Jamie Guest, May 21, Chicago Tribune

Chicago police are searching for a 27-year-old man who went missing three days ago in the Ravenswood neighborhood on Chicago's Northwest Side.

Thomas Soldano was last seen May 17 and reported missing May 20 by his roommate, Karl Dabney. Dabney reported having seen Soldano in the early morning hours of May 17, just before Dabney left for work in the Chicago Loop. Dabney said that when he returned home, Soldano was missing from their shared apartment in the 3800 block of N. Ravenswood Avenue. Soldano's clothing and personal belongings were taken, but no note or forwarding address was left.

Dabney said it was unlike his roommate to disappear for several days without responding to phone calls or text messages. Repeated calls to his cellular phone went unanswered.

Soldano's sister Amanda Price, who lives north of her brother in the Rogers Park neighborhood, has been unable to locate or reach her brother.

Both Dabney and Price appeal to the public for any information regarding his whereabouts.

Soldano is described as a 5-foot, 6-inch, 140-lb Caucasian with green eyes, shaved head, and a goatee. He was last seen wearing jeans, a Columbia College red hooded sweatshirt and sneakers.

Anyone with information should contact Detective Sergeant Rose Salazar of the Chicago Police Department's Missing Persons Bureau.

Chapter One

I had been mesmerized by the apartment for months, perhaps years, on my Brown Line L train ride from Western Avenue to downtown Chicago. The place was hard not to notice, even in a city as big and crowded as Chicago. Unique things tend to stand out.

The loft apartment took up the top floor of a storefront building. Every time I passed it, I caught my breath just a little. I mean, I couldn't help but stare at the soaring glass wall that fronted one side of the unit. It was a voyeur's dream—or maybe an exhibitionist's? It certainly grabbed my attention.

Sitting on the train, I would peer into the apartment, but curiously enough, I never managed to catch a glimpse of anyone who lived there. With its openness, it had the look and feel of a movie or stage set. Every time the train went by, I would look up from whatever I was reading to simply see if I could glimpse anyone in this place that had taken on such a weird fascination for me. I desperately wanted to see the person or people who lived there. Even though it was irrational and maybe even a bit stalkerish, I wondered about who they were, what their lives were like, what drew them to this unusual apartment. Or maybe it was a condo?

It had to be one of the most unusual homes on the North Side of Chicago. The loft was just one big, open room with an open stairway up to a mezzanine, where the bedroom would be. The steps were simple wood slats with a streamlined railing made of steel cable. The wall opposite the soaring glass was exposed brick, distressed, dripping mortar between the red bricks. Simple. Minimalist. Almost industrial. Ductwork was visible, silver, and a little bit corroded.

It had hipster charm for days.

I often imagined that, despite it being so open to prying L-rider eyes like mine, I would love to live there. There was something both magical and magnetic about the place. I longed for the day when I would roll on by and see a FOR RENT or FOR SALE sign affixed to the glass.

I think I even dreamed about it a time or two.

Even though I never saw them, my imagination worked overtime to visualize the people who lived there. I imagined an artist or maybe a sculptor, someone creative anyway. I'd put myself in his or her place, hoping one day I would have the opportunity to move around that large inviting space, to tiptoe up the stairs to the loft in the evening, to cook a meal in the small kitchen, to gaze out as trains rumbled by, sparks from the rails in their wake.

Inspired.

I never imagined my dream would come true.

But it did. And in a funny way, what drove me to this particular apartment led to a lot of dreams coming true.

But dreams can turn to nightmares in the space of a single breath.

Fate stepped in one day and changed everything—past, present, and future—when I rounded the bend of the L tracks and my glass-walled apartment came into view.

On that day, there was a change, a difference of two words.

Hanging as though suspended in midair was one of those black-and-red signs one can buy at the hardware store. The sign proclaimed: FOR RENT. Below the bright red letters was a white rectangle with a phone number written in black marker.

Oh my god. It's coming true. This place will be gone by the afternoon! I can't let anyone else have it.

I dug inside my messenger bag, groping for paper and pen to jot down the number. I'd call the moment I got to work, already feeling like I was racing against some imaginary clock hanging just above my head. Such a unique place wouldn't be on the market for long. Hell, someone else might have already snatched it up.

I wasn't fast enough to write the number. Of course, I wasn't. The train had stopped for only a minute, two at the most, long enough to let a few folks off and a whole bunch on. There was a lot of chatter, the huffing of the train, the pneumatic hiss of the doors closing, and the garbled announcement for the next stop.

The apartment—and the FOR RENT sign—sailed by as it always did, and the phone number along with it. I turned in my seat, straining to try to see the number from this distance, even though I knew it was a stupid and impossible move.

I knew, as sure as anything, if I waited until the next day, with my pen poised and ready over a pad of paper, the sign would have vanished. Someone else would take possession of what I felt, in a weird and possessive way, was rightfully mine.

There was only one thing to do.

I tried to be patient despite my thundering heart, waiting until we neared the next station. I leapt up and edged my way through the crowd toward the doors. When they slid open, I stepped out and stood on the platform, giddy with my own impulsiveness. This wasn't like me. I was usually a planner, every decision carefully considered before moving forward—or not.

Impulsive was something other people did.

On the platform, I paused for a moment, watching the southbound Brown Line train as it continued its journey toward the Loop. In the distance, the skyscrapers of downtown rose. A breeze rustled my hair. Autumn was definitely present, even though the sun peeked out through scattered clouds, drifting downward in illuminated shafts, like a religious painting. There was an undercurrent of chill that, at the time, I attributed to nothing more than the changing of seasons.

But now I wonder—was the chill an omen, foreboding? Was fate trying to tell me to get back on the next train and get to work like the safe and dependable guy I was? After all, I had a home and in it was a man I loved, a man to whom I hadn't even whispered a word about wanting to move.

It was late autumn in Chicago and the day had all the portents of the coming winter. Gray, low-hanging clouds amassed near the horizon, some of them so dark they verged on black.

In the short time I stood there, the weather made a dramatic change, which, if you've ever visited Chicago, you know isn't unusual. "Don't like the weather?" Self-proclaimed wits were fond of saying about the Windy City. "Stick around for a few minutes, and it'll change."

The little sun there was vanished, beating a hasty retreat behind a bank of fast-moving and bruised clouds. Drizzle hung in the air. A needling, cold mist crept into my bones, making me shiver. This was worse than a downpour because it seemed like no matter how much one bundled up against it, the cold seeped into one's bones, making it nearly impossible to get warm. The wind, which blew off the lake two miles east, picked up, running at a breakneck pace, westward bound, down Irving Park Road. I watched from the platform as the people below rushed to get out of the inclement weather, their umbrellas turning inside out. The wind ripped the last of fall's leaves from their branches.

In spite of the weather, I made my way along the old wooden L platform to its northern end so I could stand directly in front of the object of my desire.

It was the first time I'd actually seen it up close. And now it almost looked unreal, as though it were a movie location dreamed up by the guy who did the set for Hitchcock's *Rear Window*. My current view had that same urban, surreal feel, that same voyeuristic quality.

Looking back, I wondered if it also had that same air of menace Hitchcock was so noted for.

Close up the apartment *was* different.

I admit—I had idealized it. The soaring glass wall that I was so taken with was actually part of the roof and the glass had metal mesh inside it. I had imagined pristine glass; this was marred by water and mud stains, the color more a translucent gray than clear.

But I could still see inside the apartment, which looked quite small, but interesting: it was all one room, on two levels, with a large living area and kitchen down, and the sleeping area up. I don't know if the current tenants were in the process of moving out or if they were simply minimalists. The place contained only a platform bed on the upper level and a swooning couch on the lower.

Whoever, they were, I decided, they lived much of their home lives horizontally.

I liked that.

And then I noticed one more thing—an elaborate screen pushed to one corner, near the wall that could be called the kitchen because of its stove, refrigerator, cupboards, and sink. Even through the rain-smeared glass and in the dim light of a rainy autumn morning, I could make out that the screen had been elaborately painted in a kind of graffiti style that reminded me of Keith Haring. Lurid red, white, and black leaped out at me from across the way.

I first heard and then saw the approach of another southbound train. I knew I had time to write down the phone number written on the FOR RENT sign, but inspiration, or fate, stepped in once more.

Why not just get off the platform, descend to street level, and see if I can claim this little piece of home right now?

Because my confession to not being very impulsive was somewhat true, I did take the precaution of jotting the number down.

And then I turned and descended the steps off the platform and continued through the turnstiles. Once I was in the relatively quieter environs of the Irving Park Brown Line L station, I pulled out my cell phone and called the number.

It took me by surprise when a woman picked up on the first ring. *It's almost like she was sitting by the phone, waiting for me to call.* I'd expected to leave a message, so for a moment, I was a little taken aback, tongue-tied.

When I could engage brain and mouth, I said, "I'm calling to inquire about the apartment for rent."

As soon as I said the words, I had the eerie feeling that I'd crossed a line. Nothing was ever going to be the same again. The words tumbled out and even then there was something within me, something no logic or reason can account for, that caused me to inexplicably *know* my fate was about to change and my wish for that apartment, placed into the universe subconsciously over many, many morning trips to work, was about to be granted. There was also a moment where an almost irresistible force compelled me to simply hang up, let go of this dream. Following it was rash, impulsive.

Before the woman even continued speaking, I knew I would be moving into that apartment the first of November. Even as the woman, her voice chipper and upbeat, perhaps a bit *too* friendly, invited me to come and have a look at the place right then, another thought, a clichéd one, intruded: *Be careful what you wish for.*

"I can be there in ten to fifteen minutes, depending on traffic. Twenty, maybe, it *is* rush hour after all."

"No worries. There's a coffee shop across the street from the L station. I'll just hang out there until you get there."

"Oh, Matilda's?"

I glanced over at the hand-painted sign on the storefront window. "Yup. That's the one." The place actually looked inviting, what with the damp and the temperature plunging downward. Snow was not unheard of in Chicago in October. I imagined I could smell the approach of a few flakes on the draft riding into the train station.

"Say hi to Dorothy, if she's working. And grab yourself a cinnamon roll with your java. They're to die for. Better than Ann Sather's."

"That's a tall order—" I started to say because Ann Sather's Swedish restaurant a few stops south, on Belmont Avenue, was famous for their gigantic and super-delicious rolls.

But the woman had already hung up.

I said to my dead phone. "And your name is? What will you be driving? *Will* you be driving? How will I recognize you?" I laughed at myself and powered off my phone, slid it in my pocket, and headed outside.

The cold wind nearly took my breath away as I hurried across the street and into Matilda's. Inside, the windows were steamed up, but it was warm. The espresso machine hissed noisily. Jazz tinkled softly over the sound system and I recognized Oscar Peterson's piano. The song was "Night Train."

I stepped up to the counter and a rail-thin woman with her salt and pepper hair pulled tightly away from her face hurried over from the machines to take my order. She looked more like Auntie Em than Dorothy.

I smiled. "Are you Dorothy, by any chance?"

"You mean as in Gale?"

"What?"

"Dorothy Gale? Toto, we're not in Kansas anymore? Follow the yellow brick road!"

I guffawed. "Um, no. Someone just told me to say hi to Dorothy."

She narrowed her dark eyes at me, almost as though she thought I was pulling her leg. "You mean Dorothy Bartsch, I think. But whoever told you that was putting you on. Dot passed away a couple of years ago. Stroke. She used to own this place with her wife, Matilda. Matilda's in Naperville now in an assisted living joint." She sighed. "But that's probably TMI when you just want your caffeine fix, right?"

"I'm sorry."

She waved my apology away. "What can I get you? The Sumatra is excellent."

"I'll take that." I pondered for a moment, my sweet tooth clamoring for attention, so I added, "And a cinnamon roll."

"Sorry, hon. We sold the last one half an hour ago. Morning rush. We'll have more in the afternoon."

I laughed. "I didn't need it, anyway."

"We still have the pecan rolls if you want one of those? A donut, maybe?"

"Just the coffee, please."

"You want room?"

"Nah." I was tempted to add the old chestnut, "I like my coffee like I like my men. Black." But one never knows how such jokes might be taken in our PC times even though the line was quite true in my case.

Once I had my coffee, I meandered with it over to the window to wait for the mystery woman who would hold the key, maybe, to the apartment—and my future. *Our* future. Me and, as Sophie Tucker might say, my boyfriend, Ernie's. I hopped up on a stool, set my coffee on the little wooden bar bisecting the window, and wiped the steam away with the wrist of my jean jacket.

I waited for ten minutes, maybe a little more, when I saw her hurrying down Ravenswood Avenue from the north, head bowed against the wind. Something instinctive and prescient assured me, without a doubt, this was the woman I'd spoken to on the phone. She wore a beige raincoat, bright orange rubber rain boots, and had a mane of wild and frizzy red hair. Her glasses were rain-splattered and fogged. I wondered how she could see. She paused at the front door to clean her glasses and fluff her hair—which made it look exactly the same as it had before. If this were a movie, Diane Keaton would play her.

I turned on my stool a bit as she entered the restaurant. Out of the corner of my eye, I observed her looking at the chalkboard above the counter, and then her gaze landed on me.

She smiled. I grinned back. She was an odd character, but attractive in a weird sort of way. Her eyes were an arresting shade of green and the irises were magnified by the big round tortoiseshell-framed glasses she wore. This one was probably close to blind without her specs. Her hair framed her pale, freckled face in a way I'm sure a straight guy would find alluring. She had that kinda sexy librarian vibe.

She took a longing last glance at the counter and came over to me, hand extended. "You're the guy who wants to look at the studio on Ravenswood? I didn't catch your name."

I hopped down from my stool so I could shake hands. "It's Rick. Rick D'Angelo. And you are?"

"The real estate lady?" She laughed. "I'm hedging because no one believes me when I tell them my name. My folks had a perverse and, I might add, a very cruel sense of humor."

"Okay."

She seemed flustered. "It's Olive."

"That's not so weird." I shrugged. "A little old-fashioned, maybe, but normal. I like it."

"Wait until you hear the last name."

"What is it? Green?" I chuckled.

"Close. Branch. Olive Branch." She eyed me and then held up a hand. "I don't want to hear another word about it."

I was relieved. What can you say anyway when there's an olive branch right in your face?

"I don't have a ton of time, Rick, so if it's okay with you, let's go check the place out."

I followed her outside. The rain had slowed to a drizzle, which wasn't unpleasant.

We traversed the short distance to the industrial building I'd looked at from the L platform. There was a storefront at ground level that was closed, and I wasn't sure it was still even in business. It was one of those places that sold ready-to-assemble hardwood furniture that you'd need to sand and stain or paint yourself. I didn't see the appeal.

"They're out of business." She nodded to the furniture store, pointing out the obvious. "The unit's pretty quiet." Grinning, she added, "You get used to the trains. After a time, you won't even hear them." Olive unlocked a side door and swung it open. I followed her up a narrow staircase. The hallway had a musty odor. "Sorry about the smell. Someone needs to open a window."

We got to the top and I thought I'd die of impatience as Olive fumbled finding the keys to the front door.

After a few mumbled tsks and curse words, she found the right key and turned it in the deadbolt. She swung the door open and stepped aside to let me enter.

As I walked in, I had an odd sense of déjà vu. I suppose I could attribute it to seeing the place from the train, but the sensation gave me pause.

It was akin to stepping through the looking glass. I mean, I'd peered into this very same space for so long that I felt as though I knew it. Perhaps my knowledge was a snippet left over from a dream...

I took it all in, trying to ignore the feel of Olive's gaze on me.

The place looked familiar, yes, but also felt different. Smaller, maybe. There was the open staircase up to the loft. Here was the little kitchenette, looking more run-down than I would have imagined. The Formica countertop was scuffed and the chrome trim held spots of rust. The white porcelain sink bore brownish stains, probably from the steady drip, drip, drip of the tap. The cabinets, which I had assumed were painted white wood, were actually white metal and they too had a few spots of rust, like a cancer. Still, I told myself they'd be functional.

I looked up, marveling at the black stamped-tin ceiling, at least fourteen feet above us. Vintage.

The floor was old parquet, oak, scuffed, and in need of refinishing. Dust motes danced in the air in the sparse sunlight filtering in through the wall of glass.

I closed my eyes for just a moment to breathe in the place's essence, to solidify the fact that I was finally here. While my eyes were shut, I felt Olive's hand on my shoulder for just a moment—a light squeeze and then gone.

I opened my eyes and turned to look at her.

She was at least ten feet away near the glass wall, head cocked and—I suppose—trying to gauge my reaction to the place.

I shuddered. *It was just your imagination, that's all.*

I moved a little toward her, looking out over her head at the view outside once more.

Olive must have seen me gazing toward the window because she said, "Privacy. You're thinking about privacy."

She pointed to the red and black screen I'd viewed from the train. Close-up, it looked like someone had taken part of a graffitied wall, framed it, and stood it up in here. "The previous owners left that behind, so it helps. Comes with the place, if you want it. Or I can have it taken away. But people are going by too quickly on the train to really pay much attention." She shrugged. "These days, everyone's looking down at their phones all the damn time anyway."

"Ain't it the truth?" I agreed softly. My own phone vibrated in my pocket. It was probably my boss, wondering why I wasn't at work. I didn't bother to check, but did a quick tour of the place. The bathroom was vintage, with black-and-white tile floors and a clawfoot tub with metal piping around the top to enclose it for showering.

I was just about to turn and to tell Olive I needed to get a move on, when I caught movement out of the corner of my eye. I turned quickly and saw the back of a person—not Olive—reflected in the mirror. I blinked.

There was nothing there, of course.

In spite of this, I told her, "If you don't have a long line of takers, I'd be interested in a lease."

Ernie is going to kill me.

"I knew you would. It's a unique property." She dug in her voluminous orange leather bag and pulled out a credit application. "I was ready for you."

She smiled.

I ignored the fact that I sensed something predatory in that grin.

Before: The Detective

Chris Hanson had worked for the Chicago Police Department for more than twenty years, ever since he graduated from the University of Illinois, Chicago Circle, with an associate's degree in criminal justice. The last three years he'd spent in missing persons, and he'd found that time the most depressing and yet, the most rewarding stint of his career.

Depressing because his cases often had ugly resolutions. Missing young people turned up dead. Or they'd left homes where they were, in one way or another, abused or neglected, and they were desperate to get away, at any cost.

Most depressing of all? The many, many cases that led nowhere. A missing soul vanished off the face of the earth and was never seen again. It was the cruelest outcome for those left behind because there was no end, not even a tragic one, to their personal stories. There remained only questions and an ache of longing to know something time and circumstance stubbornly refused to reveal. In cases like those, the presumption of death was the most common explanation. But when a person—or even their remains through whatever machinations—

disappears without a trace, it casts a darkness that may never become illuminated again.

Of course, people who disappear never to show up again have most likely left this mortal coil, but if there's no proof of that, hope can linger for years after the disappearance. Do they have amnesia? Were they being held captive? Who knew? And that was the problem.

Chris's boss, Melody Shapiro, had just left his office. Her words, matter-of-fact, yet true, echoed. "You need to let this go. There are far too many missing people out there to expend the power, time, and resources to continue to follow up on Thomas Soldano. I'm sorry, Chris, I know your heart is in the right place, but we can only do so much. We have other families and friends to worry about, to help find a resolution."

Melody, a tough-talking, no-nonsense, steel-haired woman of fiftysomething, always came down on the side of practicality. Dozens, maybe more, folks went missing every day from the Chicagoland area. Most were found within a day or two, sleeping off drug or drink binges, seeking respite from people they live with whom they saw as abusers, or simply forgetful folks who didn't leave a message and let their phones die. But when they didn't show up in forty-eight, seventy-two hours, Missing Persons became more concerned.

But Melody, at least, with her logic-dictated instincts, prioritized the missing by who they were when they were last seen. For example, last spring, when Senn High School senior Rebecca Montrose vanished one day on her walk home from school, Melody was in favor of pulling out all the stops to search for her. Rebecca was "a good girl," a gifted student, class treasurer, and president of the Latin

Club. Her parents, whom they had no reason to doubt, underscored their daughter's punctuality and how she *always* would call, even if she was going to be as little as fifteen minutes late.

Despite running down too many leads to count, organizing neighborhood searches, and more, Rebecca Montrose was still among the missing.

But Thomas Soldano? Not so much. Melody had told Chris, "Let it go. All signs point to a drug-addicted loser. He was heavy into crystal and you know what that does to people. Turns Jekylls into Hydes." Melody shook her head, eyeing Chris all the while. "I know you think there's more to the story. But chances are, Chris, there's nothing more than someone out of his speed-freak head holing up and bingeing in some cheap motel or with another tweaker. Sad but true, bud. Move on to a worthier case."

After she'd left his office, he stared down at the snapshot of Thomas "Tommy" Soldano and a sad smile crossed Chris's face because the young man reminded him of his own young son, Jeffrey, lost a couple of years ago to heroin.

Tommy had Jeff's smile and his wide-set eyes. Chris could see the little boy Tommy had been in his mind's eye and it induced an ache in his heart. He looked down once again at the snapshot, taken at a Lake Michigan beach on what must have been a very hot summer day because blankets and beach towels were nearly touching, they were so close together. Tommy was smiling and waving at the camera, wearing red-and-black board shorts and a pair of aviator sunglasses. His hair was caught by the breeze, blown away from his forehead. There was a kind of casual joy to the photograph. Chris knew Tommy had fallen into addiction, just as his own son had, tragically, not all that long ago.

It had made him want to find the young man all the more.

But after a week of running down leads, some even on his own time, Chris had come up empty-handed. There wasn't a trace of the young man. It was almost as though he never existed.

His boyfriend, Karl Dabney, had given Chris the initial impression that he was as distraught as Tommy's sister, Amanda Price, over Tommy's disappearance. But in subsequent conversations, Chris grew more and more suspicious of Karl. Something was off.

Chris had been a detective long enough to pick up on telltale signs when someone was hiding something—the lack of eye contact, the fidgeting. Worst of all, Karl seemed a bit too satisfied with the idea that Tommy's case would be closed soon because of lack of evidence.

It was almost as though he expected that outcome.

Chris took one last look at Tommy's picture, shook his head, slid it back into the file and shut it. He took a moment to close his eyes. The image of Thomas Soldano was stamped on the back of Chris's eyelids. His heart ached for the young man because he knew that, whatever had happened to him, it wasn't good. He whispered a small petition that he was wrong and that, through the machinations of miracle or happenstance, Thomas would one day return and wonder what all the fuss about him was over.

Chris stood.

There were so many other lost souls waiting for him to find them.

Chapter Two

"I don't know that I can move." I groaned as I glanced over at Ernie, who set the last of the boxes down on the hardwood floor. He grinned at me in that way of his, that lazy lopsided smile that never failed to set my heart to fluttering. Even when I was bone-tired and close to collapse, that smile of his, cockeyed and sexy, could revive me.

"You're exhausted. It's understandable. I told you we should have hired movers or at least coerced some of our friends into helping us." Ernie was forever the reasonable one. He was even reasonable when I told him about renting this place before consulting him. I had been prepared for an epic battle or at least some suspicion, but he simply said, "If it makes you happy, then it makes me happy." Who does that?

I was lucky to have him, and I knew it.

"I know. I know. But movers are so expensive. And we are not made of money." I waved his I-told-you-so speech away with a weary hand. The financial comment was true—what with paying the security and first and last month's rent up front, we were essentially broke. Thank goodness our previous landlord had been understanding about letting us out of our unfulfilled lease graciously. But who was he to argue with my little white lie about Ernie's promotion—to Amazon headquarters in Seattle? "I just wanted to get it done and the quickest, cheapest way was just the two of us and a U-Haul. We're young. We're strong."

"And look at you now." Ernie's smile was kind.

I could envision what Ernie saw, me sitting against one wall, legs splayed out before me like a discarded marionette, looking like the act of drawing breath took too much effort, which wasn't far from the truth. Even my dark-brown hair, I was certain, looked wilted, plastered to my skull by sweat.

Ernie and I had been at it since early that morning, and now our east-facing windowed wall revealed twilight hues—pink and lavender near the horizon and the dark navy of night at the top. It was a stunning view until it was broken by the screeching, lumbering, sparking form of a Chicago L train as it rumbled by, making the boxes on the floor vibrate and some even slide a little on the hardwood. Oh, it was going to be fun living here! Maybe it would feel as though we were having an earthquake every ten minutes or so. Me and my impulsiveness!

To be fair, Ernie *had* thought I was crazy when I told him a few weeks ago I wanted to move here. That's what I started out with, committing a sin of omission by not mentioning I'd already filled out a rental contract and credit application. But, as I said, Ernie has always indulged me, even when it was to his detriment. Whatever Ricky wants, Ricky gets. Ernie's modus operandi had served our nine-year-old relationship well so far. I had no reason to believe it wouldn't continue to do so.

"Okay, okay, I admit it. I'm tired. Worn out. Exhausted." I breathed in deeply and let the tired air out as a sigh. To comfort and console dear Ernie, I told him, "We can unpack tomorrow."

I grinned at Ernie as he opened one of the boxes and started to sort through it. Unlike me, Ernie's fatigue had manifested itself in restlessness.

I sat up straighter, eyeing him. "Do you even know what you're looking for?"

He glanced up, as if caught at something, and laughed. "No. Just keeping busy."

"I would think you would have had enough 'busy' for one day. Come over here and sit down beside me." I patted the floor. Tired as I was, Ernie still looked mighty good. His ebony skin and tall muscled frame were packed into a pair of old ripped jeans and a Roosevelt University T-shirt, darkened at the pits, which, perversely, I found sexy.

"Said the spider to the fly?" Ernie shook his head. "Don't think I don't see that look in your eye." He stood. "No, I think I'll run the truck back to the U-Haul place before it closes. Then we won't have to worry about it tomorrow. I don't suppose you'd like to join me?" Ernie shrugged into his worn denim jacket.

"I would, but I thought I'd take care of some unpacking while you did that."

"Right! Right." Ernie laughed. He didn't believe me. Hell, I didn't believe myself. But Ernie went on, entertaining the illusion. "I'll expect to see an amazing transformation by the time I get back. Rugs unfurled. Furniture placed just so. Pictures hung. All homey and nice." He burst into laughter. "And dinner on the table. Maybe Chateaubriand for two?"

He crossed the one big room of our new home and squatted down next to me. He leaned in and kissed me. His lips were warm and his skin felt hot, smelling of musk and sweat. I pulled him in closer, hungrily. He almost lost his balance. I whispered, "The pictures might not be hung, but just be glad your boyfriend is." He stood quickly, knowing from years of experience how this scenario would end if he didn't put the brakes on.

I grinned at him, panting a little. "Go on, leave me here all frustrated."

Ernie glanced back toward the window as another train went by. "Maybe you can keep the mood alive by playing to the crowds on the train. Strip down, put on a little music, do a little dance." He leered and winked.

"Perv. Don't you have a hot date with a truck?"

"I'm going. I'm going."

I stared at the door after Ernie left, and then I leaned over and switched off the lamp on the floor next to me. The dark made the window and the railway scene just outside come to even more vibrant life. It was almost like a movie screen in front of me. Would Ernie and I ever get used to living in this fishbowl?

Had I done the right thing? Would I make the same decision if I had considered it for more than, oh, I don't know, five minutes? *Now's a fine time for second guesses!* Deep down, though, I couldn't deny that this simply felt right. We were *home*—already. I thought I'd close my eyes for a few moments, just to revive myself, and then maybe I'd at least make the good faith effort to unpack a box or two.

It felt like only moments had passed when someone jiggled the doorknob.

"Ernie!" I cried out, rousing myself from the floor, where I had just about drifted off into a wiped-out slumber. "We are not going to have the same problem with keys in this place that we had on Eastwood, are we?" I had accused my man of senility more than one time because of his annoying habit of seldom knowing where he had left his keys. Fact was, nine times out of ten, they were in his pocket. Or even his own hand.

Sighing, I brushed the dust off the seat of my pants and started toward the door. Before I reached it, though, there was the sound of a key being fitted into a lock and a click. I stepped back. "Ern—" The words died on my lips.

It was *not* Ernie coming through the door.

I gasped and did one of those takes you see in the movies, where one blinks rapidly a couple times, just to make sure that what one was seeing was real.

A chill coursed through me. The hairs rose on my neck. My mouth went dry.

A complete stranger stood in the doorway. He looked behind himself, down the common hallway, and then back into the space. He didn't seem to be aware I was only a few feet away, watching.

He was about my age, midtwenties, and stood about five-foot-six with a too-thin frame that made me want to feed him a few Giordano's pizzas. The guy had dark, buzzed hair and a matching goatee. His skin, even in this dim light, looked ashen, marred by sores in various stages of healing. He lingered just over the threshold and the weird thing was, there was the odd sensation that he—I don't know—didn't exist in the same place and time as I did. Irrational? Sure, but it's what I felt.

His dark eyes darted about our new home, as if he were looking for something, yet not seeing anything at all.

"Hello? Can I help you?" I said, standing still, licking my lips. "Hey man. Who the hell are you? What are you doing here?"

I was too weirded out to know exactly what I was feeling. I wasn't quite scared, more like stunned. In shock? I tried to assume that maybe he had the wrong apartment.

He certainly looked harmless enough. In fact, if I put enough breath behind it, I thought I could probably blow him off his feet.

He didn't answer. He continued to look right through me, as though I wasn't standing there, all six feet two inches of me. Other than stacks of boxes, rolled up rugs secured with twine, and furniture shoved at odd angles, I was pretty hard to miss, even in the orange-tinted light seeping in from our huge window.

And then he walked, a little jerky, farther into the room—right into my and Ernie's new home. *Like he owns the place. Who the fuck is this guy?*

"Hey, hey! What do you think you're doing?" I snapped. "What's the deal?" I moved a bit closer, thinking to block further entry. Should I cry out for help? Call the cops? I fingered the phone in my pocket and for a moment, wished it were a weapon instead.

There was no indication he heard me.

Dumbfounded, I watched as he continued his progress into the apartment unabated. I was too stunned to do anything but stand and watch, gnawing on a hangnail. He moved into the center of the room and did something really strange—he squatted and felt around on the bare floor, as though groping for something.

He paused for a few moments. The rest of his actions were all pantomimed. To the best of my ability, I could discern what looked like someone taking a pipe in his hands, bringing it to his lips, firing up a bowl with—again—a non-existent lighter, and then blowing out an invisible cloud of smoke. He closed his eyes and whatever his imagination told him he was smoking must have been deeply satisfying. His eyes popped open once more and he appeared all at once more alert.

I sniffed. There was an odd odor in the room—something chemical, like burnt plastic. When I sniffed a second time, though, it was gone. I'd imagined stuff before, but I'd never conjured up a smell.

At that moment, he seemed to notice me standing there. I'm sure I was slack-jawed and, to be honest, starting to get more than a little bit scared. I gripped the phone in my pocket once more, my fingers holding it so tightly I feared cramping. As stealthily as I could, I withdrew the phone from my pocket, brought up the home screen, and then pressed 911.

But I didn't hit send. Not yet.

Would anyone hear me if I screamed? Over the roar of an L train?

And if I did place a call to the cops, what would I say? Someone was in my new apartment, pantomiming what appeared to be drug use?

It was then I glanced over at the door and realized something that caused my blood to run cold.

The chain lock near the top of the door was in place. Now that I saw it, I remember pushing it into place just after Ernie left.

So how could this guy have gotten in?

"Who are you?" The words, with barely enough breath to support them, slipped from my lips.

He smiled. There was something winsome and sad in it, something plaintive in those brown eyes. There was about him the essence of a ruined little boy. Oddly, looking at him, I grew calmer. I sensed somehow that he wasn't a threat.

His teeth were repellent—how did someone so young end up with such badly decayed teeth? He held the imaginary pipe out to me and raised his eyebrows in a questioning invitation. When I didn't move, he shook the hand holding the "pipe" impatiently, as though beckoning me to take it.

"What the fuck?" I whispered. I moved toward him.

That's when the floor creaked, and I turned just in time to see a shadow cross the wall. It was fast—almost a blur. But the dark shape had a human form. For some reason, the shadow brought with it an icy chill. It was like black smoke moving across the room.

I tried to scream, but when I opened my mouth, nothing came out save for an embarrassing squeak. My voice had been sucked away. The interior of my mouth and my throat were as dry as a desert at the height of summer. I shut my eyes for a few seconds, trying to hold back the gibbering shriek lodged deep down.

And then I opened my eyes and turned back. The intruder was gone, as though the shadow I had seen a moment ago had swallowed him up.

The door rattled as someone tried to open it. If I was able, I would have screamed.

And then Ernie's voice came from behind the locked door. "Honey? Rick?"

I swam up from dream to wakefulness all at once, feeling disoriented. I was panting. I got up and crossed the room, sliding the chain lock open.

Ernie's brown eyes focused on me with concern. "Drift off? Bad dream? I heard you screaming from all the way down the hall." He looked so concerned. I felt sorry for him.

But I couldn't say anything, not right away. My tongue was still thick in my mouth.

What had just happened? It all seemed so real. I shook my head, peering around me, assuring myself that where I was now, in this moment—that was what was genuine. This was reality.

I can't say I can remember, during the course of my whole life, ever having had a dream that felt so real.

Had I really *dreamt* the little man? I must have. What other explanation could there be?

Everything that had just occurred had all the earmarks of reality, deeply steeped in the present. He *had* been here, hadn't he? The little guy with the bad teeth and the ripped jeans? He wore a Keith Haring T-shirt.

"Huh?" I stared up at Ernie. My heart hammered away, hard enough to cause me to worry about it not being up to the task. I wanted to pinch myself to ensure I was really here...that it was really now.

Ernie squatted down beside me and gathered me in his arms. "Oh my poor baby. You must have had a hell of a nightmare."

I clung to him, feeling chilled in spite of the heat radiating off Ernie's body. Burying my nose in his chest, I whimpered, "Did you forget your keys?"

He pulled back, enough, I suppose, to search my face for a sign that I was kidding. He held his keychain in front of me as proof. "No. Why would you ask that?"

I swallowed as the spit worked its way back into my dry mouth and throat. "Didn't you just leave? Like, five minutes ago?"

Ernie's eyebrows came together in confusion. "Yeah… well, about *forty* minutes ago to be exact. I'm sorry. When I went to come back, there was some kind of delay on the L. Big surprise! Three trains running express right by me. So I went down to Broadway and splurged on a cab." He paused. "Hon, you were asleep. You had a bad dream. You do get that, don't you?"

I nodded, not at all sure I did.

"What was the dream?" Ernie put a calming hand to my cheek. "You should tell me about it."

I shivered, remembering the little man who had just been here. Hadn't he? No, Ernie was right. I had just had a bad dream—yet it was so real, leaving me stunned and confused. "I don't know. It seemed like it was really happening. I thought it was you coming back. Someone jiggled the doorknob and I got up to let the person I thought was you in, but it wasn't you."

My heart, which had just begun to settle, sped up again as the image of the intruder crystallized once more in my mind. I barked out a short laugh.

Ernie let go of me, sitting down on the floor close enough so that we still touched. Into the darkness, I related the details of the dream, the man, what seemed to be his pantomimed actions of lighting a pipe, holding it out to me.

When I was done, embarrassed heat warmed my cheeks. I suppose it did sound like a dream. It was a dream; it had to be.

"Weird," was all my eloquent boyfriend could say. "See what happens when you wear yourself out like that?"

"I see." I sat quietly for a long time, watching as one northbound and one southbound train passed. "Must have just been so exhausted. Mind playing tricks..."

Finally, I let my head loll on Ernie's shoulder and spoke softly. "What if it wasn't a dream?"

"What you talkin' about, Willis?" Ernie loved to use the vintage TV show line. He thought it was a scream. Unfortunately, no one else did. Me, I found it kind of endearing.

"I mean, what if I wasn't dreaming? What if there's some kind of leftover energy in this apartment and I just happened to see it? Maybe my being so tired put me in a place where I'd be receptive to such things."

"Oh, don't go all *Twilight Zone* on me now. What do you think? You saw a ghost?"

"Not a ghost. Just a fragment, you know?"

"Um, no." Ernie shook his head.

"Like maybe someone who lived here before. You know. People can leave energy behind." I didn't say it, but I thought it—especially dead people. I shivered.

"Hon, you were asleep. You didn't *see* anything."

I sighed. I guessed he was right.

Shouldn't I feel relieved? But even if I hadn't seen a ghost or some misplaced psychic energy, I still had trouble convincing myself I hadn't actually seen *something*. Ghost or not, the image of that man coming into the apartment haunted me, no pun intended.

"You wanna go get something to eat? I think we've done enough for one day. No need to burden ourselves with making supper. There's a horrible cheeseburger and hot dog place down the street that looks fabulously unhealthy and just perfect." Ernie grinned at me, and I knew he was trying to make me feel better by appealing to my taste for fast food.

But right now, fast food and bright lights, maybe some noisy teenagers, sounded very good, very real.

"Let's go."

Before: An Email to His Sister

from: Karl Dabney <Dabney1978@gmail.com>
to: Amanda Price <APrice27@yahoo.com>
date: May 20, 8:51 AM
subject: Tommy
mailed-by: gmail.com

Hey Amanda,

Just dropping you a quick note to see if you've
heard from Tommy. He was in bed when I left the
apartment the other morning. When I got home,
he was gone. His closet and drawers were empty,
yet he gave no indication he was going anywhere.
He didn't leave a note. You probably know all of
this already.

What has me worried is the fact that he isn't
picking up calls or answering texts. Now, you may
or may not know we've had our share of problems,
especially lately. And yes, Tommy has taken off for
the night before.

But he's never been gone for days like this. And he
always answers texts and picks up his phone—or
at least gets back to me relatively quickly.

So, I'm worried.

If you know anything about where he is or have heard from him, please let me know ASAP. I'm going to head into the police station pretty soon here to file a missing person's report, but if you know something, you can save me the trouble. I doubt they'll take me seriously, since he's a grown man and has had his share of troubles, anyway.

Give me a call either way, okay? I know you and Tommy haven't really spoken for a while, and a lot has changed with him. Stuff you probably should know. Or maybe not.

Just hoping and praying our Tommy is okay.

Love ya,

Karl

Chapter Three

Ernie would be pleased.

I had worked all day getting the place ready for his return from work. I started by shoving the furniture, rugs, and boxes to alternating sides of the big room that was our new home and cleaned the hardwood floors until they gleamed. Sure, the floor was still scuffed and in need of refinishing, but it was now at least free of dust and grit. I have to brag that I'd even managed to coax a bit of shine out of it.

I'd spackled holes in the wall, smoothing them with sandpaper, and, when they were dry, touched them up with white paint. I got the kitchen set up, organizing glassware, cutlery, dishes, pots and pans, and utensils. The sink and counters now gleamed. The bathroom smelled like pine and the floor and tub revealed not even one speck of dirt. The thing I loved about cleaning is that one's hard work paid off—there were reasonable and easily achievable goals.

I also cleaned the glass walls, using a mop and bucket to reach as high as I could. The results there were less than stellar, but I reminded myself that I had done my best, which was all one could hope for. The glass wall was still a very cool feature of our new home.

And then I set to work unpacking boxes, arranging furniture, laying our odd assortment of rugs (everything from braided to faded and worn Orientals to bold contemporary patterns that somehow worked together). Finally, I hung our meager collection of art, mostly framed posters from Ikea and photos of Ernie and me on our travels (Palm Springs, Santa Fe, New York City, Niagara Falls), in just the right places.

It now looked and felt like home, and I savored the exhaustion of a job well done. I knew Ernie would appreciate my hard work.

By the time late afternoon arrived, with its long shadows and dusky rose light, and I turned on some table lamps, the place had a genuine warm and inviting vibe. Satisfied, I poured myself a glass of the Syrah Ernie and I had opened the night before and collapsed into the overstuffed couch we had covered with a dark blue velvet blanket. I put my feet up on the old mahogany trunk we used as a coffee table.

I sighed with the contentment. If my muscles weren't so sore, I would have reached over and patted myself on the back.

Ernie would be home soon enough from his job downtown, where he worked as a tech guy for a professional association, keeping their computer systems updated and running. He was practical in a different way from me. Numbers, formulas, and making sure things were running flawlessly were attributes he embraced and lived by. I was more practical when it came to more homespun stuff, like keeping the larder stocked and the towels and bedclothes in clean rotation. We got along well—we complemented each other.

Ernie though, called me a "creative type" or "quirky." Sadly, my Chicago Art Institute education in visual arts was being wasted in yet another dead-end job at a silk screening company on the Northwest Side that made and sold custom designed T-shirts. For my efforts, I made the princely sum of fifteen dollars an hour. What I did appreciate about my low-paying, wage-slave job was that it offered decent healthcare benefits, and they were generous with time off. This latter perk was what allowed me to stay home this week so I could make our new place a perfect little nest. You take what benefits you can get, right?

As soon as I finished my wine, I'd start on a special homecoming dinner, simple but elegant—some grilled salmon atop a bed of linguine tossed with basil, capers, and lemon—laid over a bed of fresh arugula. Ernie and I may have been poor, but we ate well. I would put on some mood-setting music; I was thinking Duke Ellington or maybe Count Basie—and looked forward to truly christening the new place in style.

I was grateful the previous tenants had left behind that privacy screen, which was mobile and would shut out prying eyes from travelers on the L. No telling what Ernie and I would get up to behind that screen!

I had just let my head loll back on the couch, the delicious blackberry aftertaste of the wine in my mouth, when my momentary peace was broken by a knock on the door. Three sharp raps. I sat up straighter, pinching my arm to make sure I was truly awake. Had my little man phantom returned? The thought didn't amuse me. Instead, it gave me a nauseating chill. I got up and crept over to the door, half expecting it to open of its own accord and my unwelcome visitor from the night before to enter.

The knock sounded again. As I neared the door, I realized whoever was on the other side had the good manners to wait until I actually opened the door. This alone gave me hope that whoever was out there was made of flesh and blood and *not* ectoplasm. I glanced through the peephole and a distorted woman's face leered back at me—the nose seemed absurdly long and almost canine, the eyes tiny and porcine.

"Just a sec." I opened the door a crack and was relieved to see the woman on the other side was not nearly as monstrous as the peephole made her out to be. She was older than I was; I would put her, generously, at fortysomething. She had a broad, kind face, warm green eyes, and a riot of curly red hair streaked with gray that looked absolutely untamable. At least with regard to her hair, she reminded me of Olive Branch. A big multicolored caftan hid her large frame. She looked funny—and I mean that in a good way, in the sense that I knew, even before she spoke, she'd have the power to make me laugh.

"So you're home?" Her voice carried with it a bit of a Bronx accent. She pushed her black-framed glasses up her nose.

"Yeah. Did you always have a flair for the obvious?" I laughed to let her know I wasn't being mean.

"I always had a flair for baking, dumb ass. That's it." She rolled her eyes and grinned. "I'm Paula Prentiss, your new neighbor." She shifted the tea-towel-covered dish she was holding to her left hand, so she could extend her right.

We shook.

"You know, like the actress? *Stepford Wives*?"

I shook my head.

"Paula Prentiss? *Where the Boys Are?*"

I shook my head again and added, "I believe the boys are down on Halsted, maybe at the Steamworks baths?" I chuckled.

She waved me away. "Ah! You're way too young, honey. Anyway, I brought you and your man some of my special apple-raisin-cinnamon muffins." She held the plate out to me and I took it. "People don't welcome their neighbors enough in this world, so I try to do my part, you know?" She cocked her head, waiting, I suppose, for me to agree.

"This is really nice of you." I stepped back and held the door open wider. "Do you want to come in? I just opened a bottle of red wine."

She pinched my cheek and waltzed right in, a cloud of something that smelled like patchouli trailing her. "A boy after my own heart. I'm gonna like you."

She made herself at home on the couch and looked around. "Nice. Looks about a 110 percent better than how the last guys who lived here had it." She snorted. "They were pigs." She thought for a moment. "But lovable piggies."

I was getting ready to ask her about them, but she blurted out, "I hope you're not gonna keep a girl waiting for that wine."

"Right away." I poured her a glass, refilled mine, and sat beside her on the couch.

"Thanks." We clinked our glasses together and Paula said, "Welcome to the 'hood."

She took a swallow like the wine was water and burped behind a manicured hand. "Good stuff." She turned to me. "So what's your name? What's your story?"

"I'm Rick D'Angelo. I just moved over here—all the way from Eastwood Avenue in Ravenswood, a vast journey of about two miles. I'm a graphic designer."

She looked around the place again. "I can tell you got an artistic eye. I should have you take a gander at my place, see if there's anything I can do to make it look classier. On the cheap, of course. I don't make a fortune working the cosmetics counter at Nordstrom on Michigan Avenue, you know."

I wanted to laugh out loud at this woman, not in a way that would ridicule her, but just to let her know I appreciated her effusive warmth and humor.

"I'd be happy to. Which apartment is yours?"

"Just down the hall. I'm your next-door neighbor. You ever need a cup of sugar, you know where to come."

"Thanks. I'll keep that in mind."

"Hold on. I didn't mean you should grace my door if you need to borrow anything domestic. I just used the last of the sugar to bake those muffins. For your convenience, there's a 7-11 down the block. There, you can get yourself a hot dog, doughnut, and a pack of smokes. A complete meal, you know."

I smiled and took a sip of my wine and got back to the question I'd wanted to ask. "So, you knew the guys who lived here before?"

"Oh yeah. Tommy and Karl." She took a sip of her wine. "They were friends of Dorothy just like I'm assuming you and—what's his name—are. Correct me if I got the wrong idea, but you just don't see too many straight guys living in a studio together with one bed." She snickered.

"His name is Ernie. I'm still waiting for him to pop the question, but you didn't hear that from me." I took a sip of wine and just to be clear, said, "And yes, we're a couple."

"A couple of what?"

I rolled my eyes and Paula put a placating hand on my thigh. She had bright red nails so long they curved at the tip. "Sorry, hon, I meant no offense. If it weren't for gay guys, I'd have no friends at all!" She snorted. "But don't you dare call me a fag hag. Lord, I hate that term."

"So, what were these guys—Tommy and Karl—like? Why'd they move away? This is such an unusual place. I've had my eye on it for a long, long time."

At my question, Paula's face grew dark. Her eyes took on a faraway cast. She wasn't thinking happy thoughts.

She drained her wine glass. I was pretty safe in assuming she was doing so to buy herself some time. It was obvious I had touched a nerve.

She held out the glass. "How 'bout a smidge more?"

"Sure." I poured her some more wine and sat back down.

Paula shrugged. "I don't know. They were nice enough when they moved in a couple years ago. But then they got involved with some bad stuff." She took another long swallow of wine. "Ah. I don't like to talk about it. Kinda painful, you know? It's awful watching two people destroy their own lives." Her gaze shifted sideways to the glass wall as yet another train rumbled by. "Ah. I've probably said too much."

I didn't feel I knew Paula well enough to press her. But I wanted to; Lord, I really wanted to. Her evasiveness only made me more curious than I already was. Bad stuff? What could that be?

So, while we discussed the best restaurants and cafes in the area and who to call for the best weed, I promised myself I'd bide my time until this Paula Prentiss was ready to talk about Karl and Tommy.

I had a sneaking suspicion one of them might have been at the root of the oddness I'd been having since we'd moved in.

*

Ernie came home late. The poor guy was tired, so I tried not to get too bent out of shape when he failed to notice all the work I'd done that day or appreciate the fine dinner I'd prepared. When Ernie gets tired, it affects his mood— so we spent a quiet first night in our new home, watching the first season of *Devs* on Hulu.

It wasn't until we were in bed and I had swallowed Ernie's load (hey, I am nothing if not selfless and giving), that I remembered to mention our new neighbor. I told him all about Paula as Ernie's breathing deepened. "She's kind of like Ruth Gordon in *Rosemary's Baby*? You know who I mean? The busybody? What's her name? Minnie?"

But Ernie had already drifted off. I turned to my side, sorry to have lost him for another day and a little sad that he wasn't 100 percent present for our evening together. Why did work have to intrude so much on real life?

Because you need to eat, sweetheart, that's why. I swore I could hear Paula answer my thoughts, right in my own head. *Good Lord!*

I snuggled down beneath the comforter and closed my eyes. Maybe tomorrow I could take the chipped Fiestaware plate she had brought the muffins on back and prod her to talk about the "friends of Dorothy" who had preceded the current ones. Paula did not strike me as reticent. Sooner or later, she'd have to spill; even from my limited knowledge of her, I doubted she could help herself.

It was the middle of the night when something caused me to jerk awake.

I immediately looked to the window, expecting to see another L train screeching by, but the tracks, at this late hour, were deserted. Besides, I was already growing used to the rumble and crackle of the L trains going by. They faded more quickly than I thought into a kind of aural background. The only time I really noticed the noise was when I was on the phone.

Right now, the apartment was dead still. When you live in the middle of a big city like Chicago, the hum of noise—voices, cars, trains, buses—fade into the background. If they didn't, I suppose we'd all go crazy.

That's why it was so unnerving that at this very moment I could have heard the proverbial pin drop. It was that quiet. I rolled toward Ernie, who, if he wasn't snoring, was at least breathing loud enough for me to hear.

But Ernie wasn't there.

Now, our new place was just one big room so I got up from the bed and moved to edge of the loft. I gave the main living area the once-over. Even though it was steeped in shadows, the streetlight outside gave it a continual orange glow. The downstairs part was empty. I looked toward our couch, no Ernie, our kitchen, no Ernie, and I finally directed my gaze to the bathroom, where the door stood open wide on utter darkness.

"Ernie?" I called. No response came back. I padded down the stairs. Along with the silence, the cold was unnerving. The apartment was heated by radiators, the old Chicago reliable, and they had been clanking and clattering as we had both drifted off to sleep. I shivered and noticed my breath came out in a puff of steam.

I would have to call the landlord first thing.

But where was Ernie? I ran back up the stairs and found the clothes I had worn before bed. The sweats and sweatshirt lay on a chair. I slid into them and pulled some warm socks on my feet.

Just in case my lying eyes had deceived me, I made a quick tour of the studio. No, Ernie had not secreted himself behind the screen, nor was he under the bed, nor hiding behind the partially open bathroom door. He was not availing himself of a middle of the night shower in the dark.

He wasn't here.

I moved to our front door, peeking through the peephole to view only darkness. I opened the door and peered out into the gloom of the short hallway. The bare light bulb, in a fixture on the wall, flickered off and on, faintly buzzing.

Besides that soft buzz, everything was silent.

In the short time we'd been here, I'd actually come to like the sound of the trains going by. When they waited at the station, they made me think of a panting beast. I liked to imagine all the different lives aboard just one train, where they were going, who they'd see, what troubled them, what brought them joy. There was a whole microcosm on each train that rushed by our place every hour of the day. Maybe someday, I'd write a book and set it on one L ride and how it changed the lives of every passenger, whether they knew it or not. Even doing something as routine as taking the L was a choice and one choice could change one's life.

I missed the sound of the trains—right now, it seemed too much time had passed since one rumbled by. The silence felt eerie and out of place.

What time was it, anyway?

I closed the door and leaned against it, frowning.

Where is Ernie?

In all our years together, I never had to worry about him cheating or doing anything on the sly. Had he gotten up when he thought I was asleep and headed out for some late-night revelry? The idea was so absurd it almost made me laugh.

Almost.

Had he had insomnia and decided to slip out for some air? I shook my head. Ernie having insomnia was about as rare as a Chicago native putting ketchup on a hot dog.

I had taken only a step or two back toward the center of the room when I noticed *him* sitting on the couch.

Not Ernie.

I put a hand to my mouth to stifle the gasp. My heart rate accelerated.

The little guy was back. Even though he was turned away, I knew it was him from his small frame and his nearly skeletal form. He had a cell phone to his ear and appeared to be hunched in on himself. He was naked.

He was talking rapidly, and as I crept up behind him, holding my breath, I started to pick up on what he said. The voice was odd, having a mechanical undertone, as though it was a bad recording being played back. In the silence of him taking an intake of breath, I imagined I could even hear the white noise of static.

"You gotta help me out here, man. I hardly ever ask you to."

I made myself a statue behind the couch, listening. I really think I could have sat right next to him, and he wouldn't have noticed. The hairs on the back of my neck rose. Goose bumps formed on my arms, and they weren't from the cold.

"No, no, I can come to you. I don't care... I'll take even a little bit. Whatever you got." He laughed and his voice was reedy, kind of raspy. It had a manic energy belied by his small and ill-nourished frame. I could see him cock his head as he listened. "Come on, dude, I really need a taste. Just something to tide me over. I got the money; you know I do. I'm always good for it, right?"

He turned and I swear he looked right at me. Our eyes locked and I felt as though I was peering into some kind of black portal where nothing lived.

And then I realized, despite the intensity of his gaze, that he wasn't looking *at* me. He was looking *through* me. The sensation made me want to scream. My knees felt weak.

The hands gripping my shoulders did, in fact, cause me to scream. "Rick?" Ernie's deep voice startled me. I whirled on him and could only imagine how wide my eyes must have been.

"Where were you?" I demanded. "I looked all over."

"Wait. What?" Ernie rubbed at his eyes, obviously still half asleep. His body looked sleek in the darkness, clad only in a pair of pinstriped boxers.

Even as I said it, reality began to trickle in. An L train whizzed by and a shower of sparks cascaded down from the tracks. "I couldn't find you. You weren't *here*." Suddenly, I had an urge to cry.

Was I going crazy?

As I suspected he would, Ernie indicated the loft with a nod. "I was right up there. Asleep." He shrugged and I hated the look on his face—he felt sorry for me. "Where else would I be?"

I pulled him close, burying my face in his warm, smooth chest, listening to the steady beat of his heart. I breathed in his essence, what I called his man funk and that, with his thumping heart, comforted me. I clutched him so hard it had to have hurt, but sweet Ernie did nothing to stop me nor voiced any complaint.

He simply patted my head. "What the hell happened? I woke up and you were just standing by the couch, staring."

I pulled away from Ernie and looked back to our couch to find—no surprise—it was empty. No short men on cell phones. Just to reassure myself, I directed my gaze toward the front door, where the chain lock was still in place. My midnight visitor had not let himself out when I wasn't looking.

Ernie ran his hands through my hair. "You were sleepwalking." He sighed. "Again."

"I guess."

"Come back to bed?" Ernie took my hand and led me upstairs to the loft. He pulled back the bed clothes and gestured for me to get back to the comfort of our flannel sheets and down comforter. He lay beside me and kissed me deeply. When he pulled away, he stared into my eyes with the kind of concern that made me appreciate once more, just how lucky I'd been to have found him. He was a good man.

He touched my cheek and said softly, "Good night once more, honey. Try to get some rest. Real rest." He lay on his back. "I'm right here, by your side. And I always will be." At last, he rolled over, away from me. In minutes, his deep, regular breathing indicated that he'd returned to sleep.

I envied him. I pulled the comforter up to my ears and tried to get comfortable, but sleep eluded me. My eyes remained open until grayish light washed our apartment with dull color, gradually defining the shapes in our home.

Lying there, I couldn't get over the sensation that even though I couldn't see him, the little man was still in the room, watching me. His gaze made me tremble and the hairs on my neck to rise. How can a figment of my imagination manage *that*?

I must have actually drifted off at some point because, at a little after five in the morning, something woke me, besides the usual urge to pee. I'd heard something. I'd been half asleep, so I couldn't put a finger on what it was. But I believed it was the sound of water rushing, perhaps from the bathroom.

I was still on edge from the vision—or whatever it was—from the night before, so I was reluctant to get out of the warm bed to tread downstairs to the bathroom. I might have persuaded myself if not for the insistence of my full bladder. After all, here I was under body-warmed sheets and a quilt my own grandmother had made, with the man I loved next to me.

Why get up?

I stiffened as I heard the familiar creak of the hot water handle in the bathroom sink. The loud noise it made was clear, even though it was down the stairs. I sighed, a little jumpy. I turned to look at Ernie, thinking, weird as it would be, to ask him to accompany me down the stairs to the bathroom. What if someone was there? Someone who wasn't a ghost? The fact we had never bothered to change the locks suddenly occurred to me. How many prior tenants were walking around with keys?

Sure. One of them just wanted to wash up before heading up to the loft to stab Ernie and me in our bed.

I realized I probably heard nothing. It was a dream remnant. My overactive imagination. Anything other than an intruder or a paranormal visitor.

Isn't that what folks always think just before they're murdered or some other awful thing befalls them? It couldn't happen to me.

I took one last longing look at Ernie, who was on his back and snoring. A little line of drool escaped the corner of his mouth. Yeah, I know some folks might see that as gross, but I found it endearing. I smiled and decided not to bother him.

I swung my legs over the side of the bed. The floor at my feet felt icy and I shivered. I got up as quietly as I could. Still, Ernie let out a little abbreviated snort—an interruption to his regular symphony of snores—and then went down a notch to simple deep breathing. I glanced over at him once I stood up and was reassured to see he was still deeply asleep.

And I swore I heard the water rushing from the bathroom below.

What the fuck?

I didn't want to go down there, but damn it, I had to pee. I shook my head, telling myself I was being foolish. Perhaps the sound I was hearing was simply the water heater kicking on. Rumble of steam heat pipes, that's all...

Perhaps it was nothing at all.

I trod down the steps to the bathroom at the bottom. I paused and my breathing came a little faster.

The bathroom light was on, the door only partially ajar.

Maybe I left the light on. I could have left the door halfway open.

I didn't remember doing either thing, but they were so inconsequential it was reasonable to assume I had and then immediately forgot. How many things like that happen to us every day? We get to work and wonder if we turned the iron off or something like that.

I crept up closer to the door, uncertain.

A thin man, wearing only a pair of Andrew Christian mesh black underwear stood at the bathroom mirror, the water running. In spite of the sexy undergarments, he wasn't sexy at all. It was the guy I'd seen before. Had it been in my dreams? That's what I desperately wanted to believe. But why was I dreaming about this guy?

He was rail thin, ribs poking out, legs matchsticks. His head had been awkwardly and unevenly shaved. There were a couple scabs on his scalp, remnants of buzzing his head too quickly, too carelessly. His dark eyes looked huge in his sunken face. He stood, peering into the medicine cabinet mirror over the sink. My own reflection, standing in the doorway to the bathroom, looked back at me. He didn't seem to be aware of my presence.

He was wiggling one of his upper front teeth, back and forth. I shuddered as he gripped it. He didn't have to pull hard—the tooth came away in his hand effortlessly. He let out a little cry and then dropped it into the sink.

I gasped as blood oozed out of his gums, rushing over his cracked lips. He stared into the mirror with horror.

And then he turned to me. When our eyes met this time, it was as though his were glowing embers, deep in shadows. This time, it felt as though he saw me. "I can't sleep," he cried. "I can't sleep." A fresh rivulet of blood gushed from his mouth and over his chin.

I wanted to scream. I took a tripping step back, my eyes shut against the terrifying vision.

When I opened them again, the guy was gone, the bathroom empty. The water was off and not a single drop dripped from the tap.

There was no blood in the sink.

But the light, which should have been now off, remained on. There was a stillness in that room I can't describe. Empty. Silent. And yet charged with a strange energy.

Am I simply waking from another dream?

I rushed into the bathroom, trying to breathe normally, to quell my shaking limbs. I quickly moved to the toilet, pissed, shook off, and then dashed out of the room, feeling pursued.

I'd wash my hands when it was light.

Before: A Visit from Amanda

"It's been six months, man. You know something—come on." Amanda faced Karl, the unhappiness and suspicion plain on her features that so resembled her brother's. She'd dropped by, unannounced, at his new apartment only a couple of miles from where he and Tommy had once lived.

She'd taken a long, hard look at Karl's new home and it made her sad. The place was soulless—little more than a furnished room.

The oddest thing about it, Amanda thought, was that there were no mementos from life with her brother. Shouldn't there be something? A framed photo, maybe? A souvenir from one of the trips they'd taken before they'd gotten involved with the drugs?

Once upon a time, when the couple had lived together, they had photographs of themselves everywhere: in frames, loose, spilling across a table, hung on walls, standing upright on a desk or side table.

Now, it was as though her brother had never existed. Anyone at all could be the inhabitant of this room. It had zero personality. It made her want to cry. It also made her anger rise. What was Karl not telling her? Amanda had known him long enough not to suspect foul play, but still, wouldn't he have some clue as to where Tommy was?

"We've been over this a thousand times, Amanda." Karl's lower lip trembled. His eyes were glassy with unshed tears. He drew in a deep breath in a barely successful attempt to calm himself. He nearly shrieked, "I don't know! I don't know where he is."

"Calm down," Amanda said, picking at her cuticles, staring straight ahead. "I'm not accusing you of anything, for Christ's sake. So there's no reason to be so defensive." Amanda knew there was a lot she *wasn't* saying. She *was* actually accusing Karl, she supposed. She did suspect him of knowing more than he let on. Whether there was something evil, something nefarious about it, she doubted, but he knew something. He had to.

At least that's what she told herself. Otherwise, she'd have no hope at all that her brother would ever be found—dead or alive. If Karl did know something, then this torture of *not* knowing could at least draw to a close. She'd lost count of how many nights she'd lain awake, wondering where Tommy could be. Or she'd dream of him and wake, breathless, grateful for even that ephemeral connection.

She saw him all over town. In a café, bar, or restaurant. Walking along the lakefront trail. Shopping at Jewel. Her hope would rise, her heart would beat a little faster.

It was never him, of course. On those darkest of nights, she'd lay there, waiting for the room to lighten in shades of gray and think, for a moment, that she'd never see her Tommy again. There was no other rational explanation, and she knew it.

But knowing a thing and accepting it are different.

She stood and crossed the room to peer out the window. Below, traffic moved north and south on Damen Avenue. The sky was steel gray, threatening rain. The whole world felt listless.

Hopeless.

She turned away, moved to a stool at the bar that separated the kitchenette from the apartment proper. She sat down on it. *Maybe I shouldn't have come. Maybe I should just leave Karl alone. Maybe I should let go of all this. Move on. Life is for the living. Blah, blah, blah.*

I can't! He was my brother, my baby brother.

In her mind's eye, she saw Tommy when they were both kids in her room, playing Barbies. Tommy always made playing with the dolls more exciting. He had such an imagination, even as a little boy of six or seven. Where Amanda simply dressed Barbie and Ken up in different clothes, Tommy involved them in the seedy side of the world. There were infidelities, unwanted pregnancies, even murders. Barbie got hit by her beach buggy and was confined to a tiny wheelchair Tommy made. Ken turned out to be gay and had been having covert liaisons with GI Joe.

Looking back, she wanted to laugh. Where did a kid of seven even find out such things? He watched too much TV, too many movies that should have been inappropriate, beyond him.

But what else was he to do? Amanda knew how, because of his love of reading and dolls, his gentle and soft-spoken nature, he was the target of bullies. He was tormented physically and emotionally every day at school.

It was no wonder he retreated into an imagined world, one where he could make everything, no matter how dire, turn out all right.

Amanda wanted to just break down and sob, let it all out. She wanted to go home, light some candles in the bathroom, and sink into a hot bubble bath.

She wanted oblivion.

But she needed this talk with Karl. They'd danced around the issue too long. No one cared anymore, it seemed, that her brother was simply gone, vanished from the world. He might as well have never existed, for all the world cared. Once, she believed she and Karl were the only people who felt any sense of loss over what had happened to Tommy. Even the cops no longer gave a damn. Amanda couldn't really blame them, not seriously. People went missing every day in a city the size of Chicago. Some were found. Some returned. Many left little traces of their tragic trajectory on this earth, leaving behind loved ones, like Amanda, to ponder forever what their fate had been.

Now, she wasn't so sure, even of Karl. He was supposed to be the one person on this earth who adored her brother as much as she had. *As much as I do*, she corrected herself, unwilling to face the worst, even as it stared her in the face.

She drew in a deep breath, swiveled toward Karl, and made a confession. "I dream of him."

"I do too," Karl said, staring at her. She saw a wounded animal.

She went on, "I always see him in the same place. A forest. Tall trees that make a canopy, blocking out the sun, even though I can tell it's day. The woods are dark with deep shadows. Dried leaves and pine needles crunch under my feet as I walk toward him. His back is always turned, but the weirdest thing?"

"What?" Karl asked, the despair apparent in his whispered question.

"The weirdest thing is that, even though I can never see his face, I know he can't find his way out. I want to help him. But every time I move closer, he moves farther away. Once, I got close enough to reach out and *almost* touch his shoulder, but he moved away. My hand fell. And then, it's always the same. I look away for a just a second and when I turn back, he's gone."

She gazes at Karl. His skin has whitened, his mouth hangs open.

"What?"

Karl shakes his head.

Amanda takes in his pallor, the way his hands tremble. She repeats herself, "It's been six months, Karl. You know something."

Chapter Four

The next morning, I lay in bed for a long time, hoping the sleep that had eluded me the night before would come back once Ernie left, like a wily lover slipping into bed after the husband has left for work. I had all the right stuff—flannel sheets, warmed by our bodies, a goose down pillow beneath my head, the comfort of steam heat warding off any chill.

But sleep, that fair-weather bastard, didn't come.

Frustrated and still yearning for rest, I got up on my elbows and looked toward the diffuse light filtering in. Rain smeared our huge glass wall. Lightning zigzagged across a gray sky, followed a few seconds later by the low rumble of thunder.

Feeling like a zombie and that I actually *was* sleepwalking, I forced myself from bed and slogged the long journey (all fifteen or so steps) down to the kitchen. Ernie had thoughtfully left a half pot of coffee, still warm. I poured myself a mug, zapped it in the microwave, and moved to the window to stare down at pedestrians as I sipped. Those without umbrellas scurried, naturally, a lot faster than the ones who were lucky enough to have them.

A flash of bright red caught my eye just outside our entrance door on the street level below. Paula rapidly opened and closed her scarlet umbrella to free it of water and then, like a dog, shook her own frizzy mane of hair. She ducked inside and, distantly, the creak and slam of the heavy vestibule door informed me she was on her way up.

Maybe, I thought, grimacing at the bitter taste of the coffee, Paula knew something that would make it clear why I had experienced odd waking dreams two nights in a row about a person I had never seen. Maybe not, but I suddenly felt determined to discover more about my predecessors.

I was fully aware she didn't want to talk about them, and perhaps her history with Tommy and Karl was painful, but something told me that knowing more about who had previously inhabited our apartment might make living there a little easier for me.

Life in our new home had certainly not gotten off to a very good start. I had to do something. Talking to Paula was about as good a place to begin as any. Really, there was no other alternative. I'd done my due diligence online, searching for Tommy or Thomas Soldano. I got a lot of hits, Facebook, Twitter, Instagram and all that social media stuff. None of the hits, though, appeared to be the Tommy who'd lived here before. There were also dozens of sites that, for a fee, would give me more info on Tommy. Some of those *did* appear to be the man I sought, but really, how would knowing his credit score or if he'd ever been arrested help?

I dressed quickly in an old pair of black jeans and a matching T-shirt, slid into flip-flops and headed toward my next-door neighbor's. In the hallway, the light bulb that had been flickering the night before now glowed steadily. I realized I'd neglected to bring along Paula's Fiestaware plate, which had been my excuse for visiting her this morning. "It might also help if you washed it before you brought it back to her," I mumbled, groping for my keys.

Back inside, I headed toward the sink and stopped. "Oh Jesus, did you do this, Ernie?"

The plate lay next to the sink, sparkling clean, without even a trace of the muffins it had held. In my mind's eye, I could see it as I left it—covered in crumbs, sugar, and cinnamon. I remembered because I was worried it would attract ants.

I shivered as a chill coursed through me. As though on cue, the sky lit up with silver light and then followed that up with a deafening crack of thunder. I almost dropped the plate.

It was about as likely for Ernie to wash a plate before leaving for work as it was for the Chicago Bears to make it into the Super Bowl, or the Cubs to the World Series. Possible, but highly unlikely. Not that Ernie wasn't clean. He was simply preoccupied getting himself off to work. He liked to sleep as late as possible and, consequently, was forever running late and harried most mornings.

I looked at the plate, so innocent, yet chilled by it.

I knew I hadn't washed it and if Ernie hadn't, who had? I broke into a hysterical giggle as I wondered if our ghost would also mop floors and clean toilets. It would be so handy!

I didn't want to consider the possibilities. I grabbed the plate and set off again. I traveled the few steps it took to bring me to my new neighbor's door. I knocked.

Paula looked surprised to see me. She opened the door wider, and she grinned. "You come to see *me*? How nice! I don't get many visitors these days."

"Actually, I just wanted to return your plate." I handed it back to her. "The muffins were delicious." Paula stepped back to admit me and then closed the door behind us.

"All the boys love my muffins," Paula said. "My muffins are moist and delicious."

"Okay," I responded. Was I living a lie? Were we all residents here of some asylum, rather than an apartment building?

I looked around. Her apartment was about what I'd expected. Crowded with thrift store furniture, scarf-covered lampshades, vintage movie posters on the walls—there was one for *From Here to Eternity*, another for *Stella Dallas*, yet another for *Twelve Angry Men*. It took me back to my little-boy days and watching old reruns of the *Mary Tyler Moore Show*. Paula's place was very much like Mary's upstairs neighbor and friend, Rhoda.

Not much bigger than our own place, Paula's did not have the benefit of our glass wall. She had only one window, which looked out onto the flat rooftop of the adjoining building, an auto body repair shop. Still, her place looked homey and warm with the lamps lit. It smelled of cinnamon and nutmeg.

A cat rubbed against my leg, and I looked down to see the fattest calico I had ever laid eyes on. She peered up at me with adoring green eyes, purring. She did a figure eight between my legs.

"That's JoAnne. She's a complete whore. Don't encourage her." Paula moved toward her kitchen and set the plate on a counter. "I was just makin' myself some tea... Earl Grey. Have a cuppa with me?"

"Sure."

"Go ahead and park yourself at the table, and I'll be mother."

I sat at an old porcelain-topped table positioned next to the window. Paula busied herself making the tea, pouring it into a ceramic pot that looked like Wedgewood, and getting together a carton of half-and-half and a sugar bowl.

She joined me. "It's nice to have company."

"No work today?"

"I have Tuesdays off. Tuesdays and Thursdays. Makes for a nice weekend." She snorted, rolling her eyes.

Paula poured and coyly asked, "One lump or two?" even though the "sugar" was little green packets of artificial sweetener in a bowl. We sipped for a while, quiet, two strangers with not much to talk about.

How could I bring up Tommy and Karl without seeming nosy? What right did I have to know anything about them anyway? But there was this lingering hunch I had—that they had something to do with my weird dreams. They had to.

I noticed, among the stacks and stacks of books scattered around the room, that several of them were on ghosts and psychic phenomena. Even the novels leaned heavily toward the occult with the holy trinity of horror well-represented: Anne Rice, Stephen King, and Dean Koontz. There were also some true crime classics, by folks like Ann Rule, Gregg Olsen, and Erik Larson.

The books were my in. As casually as I could, I asked her, "Do you believe in ghosts?"

Paula grabbed my hand and stared at me with intensity. "Oh yes, honey. I think those who have departed are all around us." Her eyes lit up. "I have studied this stuff—been to several séances, and I never miss *Ghost Hunters*. Why do you ask?"

"Well, ever since we moved in, I've been having these weird dreams."

"Tell me all about them." Paula got up and got herself a ceramic ashtray and a pack of Marlboro reds. "Filthy habit, I know." She sat back down and lit up. "You want one?" The cigarette bounced up and down in her mouth.

I shook my head. "I quit many moons ago."

"Good for you." She inhaled extravagantly, then blew the smoke over my head. "So, these dreams? You having visions?"

I told her all about them, how authentic they seemed, and of the sad little man who had appeared. "They were so *real*, it doesn't really feel right to even call them dreams. You know? They were more in the realm of waking dreams. I don't know. I haven't experienced much like this before. I'm pretty down to earth."

Paula examined the glowing end of her cigarette. Outside, there was a bright flash of pure white light and then another almost deafening crash of thunder. The cat, sitting by the table, dove under the couch. She was quick despite her size. In seconds, the drum of a steady and hard downpour made a hissing sound. Paula looked toward her rain-smeared window.

She spoke quietly. "Tell me more about this short guy." There was something in the way she said the simple sentence that made me feel like she knew what was coming.

I described him—the buzzed hair, the sores on his skin, the bad teeth, the dirty clothes, all somehow brought up to another level by large, sad brown eyes, almost like those one would see in a Margaret D.H. Keane painting.

Paula's gaze flickered away. Her own eyes became shinier. Were those tears?

And then she stunned me.

Angrily, she shouted, "Get out of here!" JoAnne emerged from under the couch and dashed toward the bathroom, casting suspicious looks behind her at both of us. Paula snorted, took a puff, and a swallow of tea. When she looked back at me, she seemed more composed. But I had seen raw pain flicker across her features, and I wondered why.

She finished her cigarette, obviously agitated, before speaking again. "You saw Tommy."

"Tommy?" I asked, even though the name was way too familiar to me now.

"Tommy Soldano. He lived in your apartment before you moved in, with his boyfriend, Karl. Like I told you." She smiled broadly, her cheeks reddened with warmth. "Oh! I used to have so much fun with those guys. They were lunatics! We used to do everything together. I drank a lot of dirty martinis with them at Big Chicks and saw a lot of bad, bad movies at the underground film festival every year. We all used to volunteer, so we saw everything—the good, the bad, and especially the ugly. Todd Verow once sat right where you're sitting." She snuffed out her cigarette, and her eyes took on a faraway cast. "Oh, man. We had some good times."

"So, tell me. What happened to Tommy and Karl? Why did they move out?"

She narrowed her eyes at me. "I'm pretty sure I told you I didn't like to talk about this." She glanced down. "It hurts."

"You did, and I'm sorry to bring it up again, but I thought maybe these dreams..." I let her complete my sentence.

"Yeah. What you saw, that sure sounds like Tommy. It has to mean something." She shook her head. "Although I don't like what it might mean."

I didn't know if we were going to dance around the issue all morning, so I decided to simply be blunt. "What happened? I don't mean to upset you, Paula, but did Tommy die?"

Maybe I *had* seen a ghost.

Paula shook her head. "Actually, I don't know. No one does. Or if someone does, they're keeping it to themselves."

I cocked my head. "What do you mean?"

Paula gnawed at her lower lip and moved the cigarette pack back and forth, as if she were debating whether she should have another one. Addiction—and nerves, I suspect—won out and she lit up. "Tommy disappeared. No one's ever found him or heard from him."

"What do you mean?"

She shrugged. "He was just gone one day. Karl claimed he had no idea what happened. That he simply woke up one morning to find Tommy gone, along with all his clothes and belongings." Paula shrugged. "Of course, there was an investigation. Tommy's family came around, especially his sister, Amanda, asking questions. She was particularly worried. She swore it wouldn't be like her brother to just walk away, no matter how bad his life had become. He talked to her almost every day."

I wasn't sure what to say. I suppose people did walk off the jobs of their lives without looking back, but it seemed like a rare thing. I had never personally known anyone who had done it or anyone who even knew someone else who had. "What do you think happened?"

Paula cocked her head. "I don't know. I wish I did. Karl and Tommy changed during the last year they were here. They changed *a lot*. And not for the better. I guess you could say I no longer knew what would be in character for either of them."

"Do you want to tell me about it?" I didn't want to press too hard. I knew that, if I did, it might just make Paula decide to send me packing. I needed to find out more.

Paula angrily exhaled twin plumes of smoke through her nostrils. "Ah! They got into that shit all you gay boys think is so much fun. Christ! I'm always pickin' up those tiny Baggies off the sidewalk!"

"Meth?"

"Yeah. Crystal. Tina. Ice. Whatever the hell you call it. I call it poison." She got up from the table and went to a chest of drawers along the opposite wall. She dug around in one of the drawers, then another. She mumbled, "Shit. Where is it?" Finally, she found what she was looking for, I guess, and returned to the table. She handed a snapshot to me.

It was Paula and two guys. One of the men was tall, stocky, with streaked blond hair and a crooked smile that reminded me of Ernie's. The other guy—well, he must have been Tommy because he was—no question—the guy I had seen in my waking dreams. A chill ran down my spine.

This Tommy was different. He was vital. Aglow. Really handsome. His skin was clear, eyes bright. His hair glistened in the sunlight, long, dark, and wavy. He had a smile that I knew must have been infectious—it beamed and radiated joy. He wasn't rail thin; if anything, he was a bit pudgy, but the weight looked good on him. He looked strong, athletic. His skin, which appeared tanned and spoke of a Mediterranean heritage, was unmarred by sores. And his teeth were perfect and white, a dazzling contrast to his olive complexion.

He was a looker. It was hard to believe he had become the sad, unhealthy-looking wraith I had seen in my dreams.

"That was taken a couple of years ago. Pre-Tina. Down at Hollywood Beach one Sunday. It was like the perfect day. We used to go there on Sundays and then head over to Big Chicks for the cookout they'd have out the back." Paula's eyes were bright with tears again. She looked at me. "Is that the guy you saw?"

I nodded. "Except he didn't look so good."

"I know. That shit ate him alive. Fast. Both of them. They were such good boys. Such a happy couple. And then they started in with that shit. At first, it was just on the weekends. Then, they stopped doin' stuff with me. They started havin' guys over at all hours of the day and night.

Missing work. Men in and out of the apartment like it needed to be fitted with a revolving door." She made a *tsk* sound. "That wasn't them. It was the drug."

Paula and I were quiet for a while. Rain pattered against the window. A driver lay on his horn.

What she told me made sense. The pantomimes I had seen could be the movements of someone smoking crystal meth through a pipe. I had never done the stuff myself, but when I was single, I'd been around guys who had. I should have figured it out sooner. And the phone call? In retrospect, what I had overheard now sounded like the desperate pleas of an addict to his dealer.

"Such a shame. I know several guys that shit has done a real number on." I tentatively put a hand over Paula's and she turned her palm up so it rested against my own. Her hand was damp with sweat, but I didn't move away. I squeezed her hand. "Was anything ever resolved?"

"No. As I said, Karl did the missing persons thing and, with Tommy's family, went through all the motions. I even helped him put up flyers on streetlights, telephone poles, and in neighborhood stores with Tommy's picture on it. Like a missing pet! There was talk of a reward, but nobody had any money." Paula frowned. "He never turned up." Her breath quivered a little as she said, "Neither did his body."

She let out a big sigh. "So a little part of me still hopes. Maybe Tommy will show up again one day, and I can give him hell for scarin' the shit out of everyone." Paula slowly shook her head and said, barely audible, "But I don't like the fact that you saw him. That can't be good."

I didn't know that I had any comforting words, but I tried. "Maybe there's just some of his energy hanging around. You know, like some sort of psychic vibration, and for some reason my dreams just tuned in on it."

Paula looked thoughtful, as if mulling it over. "It's possible." She looked faraway. The cat wandered over and Paula scooped it up and hugged it. When she looked up at me again, her eyes were red. "Ricky, I'm sorry. I got a headache. I think I'm gonna lay down."

"Sure. I get it. Again, I'm sorry if I stirred up some bad stuff for you." I hurried from the apartment. Once in the hall, I cringed as I heard Paula sobbing.

What the hell had happened to Tommy? Was I seeing his ghost? And—why me? Why was he showing himself to me? I couldn't imagine a good reason.

Before: A Dream and a Beginning

Warmth. Golden. Composed of light. It courses through his veins.

He levitates, rising up from the bed. Below him, two men slumber, limbs intertwined, eggshell-colored sheets twisted up between them. He watches them, smiling.

But it's hard to concentrate on the scene below. Even harder to concentrate since he's floating somewhere near a stamped-tin ceiling.

The heat in his veins, what he can only experience as a gilded light rushing like a river throughout him. It's too distracting to allow anything else in.

Out of the slanting sunlight, a dark hand appears and snatches him. He flies through glass.

Torn.

Bleeding.

Slammed.

He screams.

Tommy Soldano woke with a start, unsure if the scream of his dream was contained only in it, or if it leaked out into the real world.

He turned in bed as Karl opened his eyes to stare. "Bad dream?" he asked, voice thick with sleep. He rubbed at his eyes, sat up, looked around their new apartment, at the stacks of boxes scattered helter-skelter across the scuffed parquet floors.

"Yeah, I guess." Tommy sat up too. Like Karl, he leaned against the headboard and scooted over so he was next to Karl's naked body. He lightly ran a hand down Karl's chest. "Can't remember much of it." Tommy shrugged. "Floating above us, feeling really good. Looking down."

"Isn't that what happens when you die?" Karl laughed, and then his handsome features rearranged so he was serious, concerned.

"Yeah, yeah. I heard that, but I don't think that was the case here." He chuckled. "Unless we're in heaven."

"Maybe we are," Karl said, brushing his lips across Tommy's scruffy face. Tommy hadn't shaved in a couple days. They'd been too consumed with packing and moving to the new place.

Karl said, "I'm home with you. And that's pretty much heaven in my book."

"Aw. You're too sweet." Tommy shuddered as he recalled the end of the dream when it morphed into nightmare territory. He saw his pale skin, the cuts, the blood in his mind's eye.

The dark hand, giant, grabbing him. He didn't know if he wanted to fall back asleep.

He was eager for the time when the dream would vanish from his concentration, like fog chased away by sunlight.

He stretched his arms over his head. Outside, the sky was bright, the sun in full power, with only a few strands of clouds up high. An L train rumbled by. "I love our new view. So urban!"

"Isn't it cool?" Karl asked.

"Hey. There's a Vietnamese place I noticed down Ravenswood a couple blocks. They have pho. Wanna try it for lunch, or I guess it would be early dinner?"

Karl grinned. "Sure. And then when we come back, I have a little surprise for you." He winked and Tommy thought he looked impishly cute. Devilish and so sexy.

"Really? What is it?"

"You'll see."

"Come on! You know I have no patience. And you know I won't give you a minute's peace over lunch unless you tell me now."

"It's just a little something to christen the place. I got it from a buddy at work."

Tommy cocked his head and poked Karl in the ribs. "I thought we christened the place before our nap." He chuckled, remembering the intense fuck, even though they were both exhausted from being up at five a.m. to start the move across town.

"This will definitely lead us to a second christening... and maybe a third...maybe a fourth. At least, that's what my bud tells me."

"What the fuck are you talking about Karl? Edible undies? Flavored lube?"

"Better."

"You gotta tell me," Tommy said.

"Okay, okay." Karl leaned over to reach down under the bed. Tommy remembered him carefully putting his Asics running shoes down there, along with his socks, before they'd attacked each other in bed. Apparently, he was hiding more than socks. Tommy was genuinely curious now.

Karl leaned over farther, giving Tommy a tantalizing vision of his ass as the sheet slipped away. Tommy wolf-whistled.

When Karl came back up, he had a tiny glassine Baggie in his hand. He held it in front of Tommy's face, giving it a little shake.

"What is that?" Tommy had mixed feelings. His skin prickled. He actually felt a little sick. They'd never used drugs, not even pot. Hell, a couple beers when they went out to the bars on Halsted and both of them were hung over the next day. Party animals, they were not. He eyed the contents of the Baggie. Little shards in various sizes. Powder. Looked kind of like ice.

Or Drano.

"It's magic sex dust. You'll see. Let's go grab a bite and come back and give it a try. Wanna?"

"I don't know, Karl." Tommy's heart thudded. "Is that crystal meth?"

"It's magic sex dust, I told you. Don't be a stick in the mud. We'll just do it this one weekend to celebrate. I'm not suggesting we make it a habit or anything. We're not stupid." Karl leaned over and put the Baggie on the moving box next to the bed. He then leapt from bed and hopped up and down, making his dick bounce.

Tommy laughed. He still wasn't sure about using the drug, but if it would make his man happy, he supposed he could give it a try. Just to see what it was like.

What harm could there be?

Chapter Five

"How can that be?" Ernie wiped his mouth and set the napkin down on his plate. We had just finished some grilled chicken, brown rice, and a celery, apple, and Parmesan salad I had thrown together.

I'd just described my morning with Paula—and told him all about our predecessors. Ernie's mouth had dropped open a bit when I mentioned Tommy, and how Tommy was, in fact, the person in my dreams.

"That's some wild shit," Ernie said softly. "You need to get yourself back to work. I think your imagination is working overtime." He paused and added, "Instead of you."

I shook my head and stood to clear the table. I began rinsing the dishes in the sink. "I don't know. My imagination? Really? Then how do you explain the guy I saw, or dreamt, or whatever, looked exactly like this Tommy Soldano person? There's no doubt in my mind that the guy in the picture she showed me is the *same* guy from my dreams." Just the thought made my hand jerk in a spasm, caused a chill to run up my spine, like an icy finger. "It was him, Ernie. No doubt in my mind."

Ernie brought over his own plate and set it next to the sink. "Are you positive? I mean, do you think it's possible you could be *projecting* your memory onto this picture? Forcing the piece into the puzzle? People can sometimes rearrange reality to suit their own personal narratives. Maybe that's what you're doing here?" He waited for me to respond, but couldn't resist saying a little bit more, "We sometimes see only what we want to see."

A little ticked off, I picked up his plate and rinsed it, not looking at him because I didn't want him to see how angry he was making me. "It's not like that, Ernie. Give me a little credit, would you?" I blew out a sigh and stared at the wall for a moment, trying to rein in my emotions. "You know how sometimes you see someone in the street or at a club and you think it's someone you know but you aren't really quite sure? I mean, it looks like them, but something's off enough to make you doubt."

"Yeah." I could tell Ernie had no idea where I was going with this.

"Well, compare that to the other times, when you see someone and you know, without a doubt, that it's someone you know. You don't feel like you're second-guessing."

"Okay." He laughed. "I suppose."

"My point is, and I wish there was a more eloquent way to put it, is that when you know, you know. You don't question it." I shut the water off and wiped my hands on my jeans. "There's no doubt. I know what I saw."

We grabbed our wineglasses and took them over to the couch and sat down. Ernie picked up the remote and turned on the TV. I picked up the remote and turned *off* the TV.

Ernie looked at me. "What the fuck, Rick?"

"I need to talk about this. Can't you understand that?" Ernie was a good man, love of my life, but he was trying my patience. I was well aware he thought what I was describing was silliness and in his rational mind could be explained away with logic.

Ernie smiled and shrugged. "I don't know what else you want me to say. So maybe through some weird thing, you did see this Tommy person. I don't know why or how that could be, but I suppose that could be said for a lot of things. I think that we don't know half the shit that goes on around us all the time." He pondered. "People show up in my dreams all the time, I guess, that I would say I've never seen. Who's to say they're not real? And where do they come from?"

It was a good question, one for serious pondering. But I wasn't in the mood for pondering. I wanted him to at least empathize.

"What if he's dead?" I sucked in a breath. "What if he was murdered?" I had had all afternoon, by myself, to dwell on things. And it should come as no surprise that my thoughts tend toward the melodramatic.

"Oh, come on! You don't really think that? Now, you *are* being melodramatic."

It's like he can read my mind. "It makes sense, Ernie. You've heard stuff about ghosts hanging around. Why? Usually, it's because they can't move on. They can't rest because something's unresolved. Maybe this Tommy is appearing to me because he's trying to tell me something."

"Tell you what? You've watched way too many horror movies. Too much crime shit."

"You have to admit it's plausible."

Ernie took a sip of his wine, shook his head, and grinned. "I don't have to admit anything. You have zero evidence to think anything so extreme." He turned toward me. "Even from the little you shared, this guy was a flake. He was a drug addict. From what you said he looked like, I'd say he was into the meth pretty heavy. And it does sound like your pal Paula corroborates that."

"So?"

"So, I know guys who have gotten into that stuff in a big way, and it affects your brain, Rick. It makes you nuts." Ernie was quiet for a long time, as if he was considering what to say next. "Look, this happened way before I met you, but I used to get together with this guy when I was single. He was a fuck buddy; you don't know him. But he smoked that stuff. I didn't want to touch it. At first, he was a lot of fun but then, for him, it became all about having other guys over. It didn't matter what we did or how satisfied I was, he just wanted more. It was...undignified. Scary."

"What does this have to do with anything?" I cursed myself for the twinge of jealousy in my gut. Of course, Ernie had been with other guys before me. So had I. Many. Still, it hurt, irrationally I know, to have him admit it. I believed Ernie when he said this was before my time, yet I couldn't help but imagine him in bed with this other guy.

"Your honor, this goes to state of mind." Ernie raised his eyebrows. "Anyway, the last time we were together, he found this real hottie on Manhunt, you know? And he invited him over. Well, the guy was nothing like his picture. He looked more like your Tommy, so skinny his ribs were poking out. And all the time he was over, he kept talking about the voices he was hearing coming from his radiator. He thought his neighbors were piping in voices to drive him crazy." Ernie looked away, remembering. "Rick. He was dead serious."

"Your point?"

"My point is that this drug eats holes in your brain, man. It can make you crazy. Now just as likely, if not more so, is the scenario that this Tommy just faded away, went off with some other addict. It's possible that he *did* die, but not here. And I doubt he was murdered. It's far more likely he flaked out and just left. Or he OD'd. I'm sorry, but the truth is usually way more boring than fiction."

I nodded. I had to admit that what Ernie said made sense. But I still wasn't sure I believed it. I didn't know if it was my own mind rationalizing, but now when I looked back at my dreams, I saw them as more than just apparitions or figments of my imagination, but as cries for help. They were unlike my regular dreams, which were usually not so real, so set in present time and place.

Yeah, I know. Overly melodramatic. And I had a feeling that to say more would simply be arguing with myself.

I picked up the remote and pointed it at the TV. *Top Chef* would be a welcome diversion, a relief. The cooks there, at least, were cooking nothing more toxic than actual food.

*

Once again, the dream had all the earmarks of reality.

This time I was aware I was dreaming, yet couldn't do anything to wake myself, despite the realization. I felt like

I was watching a movie, and someone had glued my eyelids open so I couldn't look away.

I was not in the apartment—I was outside of it. Directly outside, on an L train, pulling into the Irving Road Station on the Brown Line. The train's engine hummed as it screeched to a stop. There was a gong sound, a garbled announcement and the doors slid open. A cold, damp wind rushed into the compartment, bringing it with it a sour, chemical smell that made me want to pinch my nose shut.

Peering through the dirty glass, I nevertheless had a perfect view into our apartment. Only it wasn't our apartment. Not now. Without knowing why, I understood that this was Tommy and Karl's place. Everything was different. Lots more furniture. Lots of junk. Clothes strewn about the place and dirty dishes in the sink.

It was night and the apartment was almost dark. The only illumination came from the light over the kitchen sink. But it was enough.

And I could see him.

Not Tommy.

Karl. I recognized him from the picture Paula had shown me.

He was crying—hunched over, his body was shaken by great, spasming sobs. His hands covered his face and even in the pale half-light, his shoulders shook and his chest heaved. He stood near the bright red screen, but now it was not where Ernie and I had positioned it by the front door, but on the upper level of the room, next to what appeared to be the bed. I could see the footboard of the four-poster sticking out of one edge of the screen.

I could also see a very white foot, looking almost as if it had been crafted from alabaster.

I felt like I was intruding on a very private moment.

The train's doors slid shut; there was the gong and the mechanical voice over the intercom announced, clearly, that Addison would be the next stop. I turned in my seat to watch as the train lurched into motion.

I pressed my hand against the glass as I watched Karl fall to his knees at the foot of the bed.

Then the apartment was no longer in view.

Before: Karl Comes to His Senses

Karl was alone in the apartment and stared out at the day. Even if their wall of glass wasn't begrimed with dust and debris from the city, he thought the day would still look grimy and sad. The sky was completely overcast, so it was a single bowl of overturned gray edging on white. The sun was a white orb hanging listlessly, offering no warmth or brightness.

Tommy was gone and Karl had no idea where his boyfriend was. He wondered if the term boyfriend even applied anymore. Just what was their relationship, anyway? They certainly no longer had anything in common with other couples they knew—unless they were also tweakers. Tommy was slipping away more and more often, with no word upon his departure and no explanation upon his return. He'd be gone for hours and sometimes even days. Karl's attempts to contact him went unanswered so many times, he'd given up on trying. He simply had to have faith that Tommy was out there somewhere and that he was okay.

He hated to think of him in the arms of another man or other men. But worse was wondering if Tommy was even alive.

He slumped back onto the futon they'd set up in the main living area. It was crunchy with dirt, old crumbs. Karl wouldn't have been surprised to see a cockroach skitter out from between one of its drab and lifeless folds.

His head ached. His vision sometimes blurred. His body felt heavy. His eyes burned with their need for sleep. Karl had been up now for three days and sleep still eluded him. Sleep had become an unrequited love, a disinterested suitor constantly sought after, but rarely caught.

He looked down at himself, clad only in a pair of athletic shorts that probably smelled bad—just like him. A whiff of his armpits right now could make him reel with distaste and disgust. He had lost more than thirty pounds over the last several months and now his ribs showed. He had what might pass for a six pack, if he weren't so overall unhealthy-looking, like someone who'd managed to walk out of a concentration camp.

Where was Tommy? Karl had his ideas. He was holed up in one of the bathhouses, entertaining gentleman callers, one after the other, because when Tina was around enough was never enough. Or maybe he'd gone to one of those adult bookstores with sticky floors and glory holes. Or maybe he was in the male adult movie theater, the Bijou, in Old Town. Wherever he was, he wasn't thinking of Karl. He was thinking only of NEXT—the next hit on the pipe, the next load he would take.

God! How had they gotten here? They'd once been lightweights when it came to the mildest intoxicants, beer or a joint passed at a party.

And now...

Could he say it? Yes, yes, he finally could.

He rose and went to the window, staring out at an uncaring world that hurried by, everyone seeming to pursue normal lives—work, families, dinner out, dinner in, holidays, birthdays, books, TV shows, movies, car rides, vacations, flirting, relationships beginning, relationships ending, family celebrations, friends hanging out—all the things that Karl used to take for granted. All the things that comprised a normal life.

All the things that slipped away when he and Tommy weren't looking because they were in a cloud of meth smoke.

He stood at the window, feeling apart from the world and finally admitted it. "I am an addict." Once the words were out, Karl felt a sense of relief. It wasn't a huge revelation, but it was as though something heavy had been lifted from his shoulders.

It felt like a start.

When, or if, Tommy came home, he'd admit the same to him and hope and pray Tommy would say the same back, much as they had once declared "I love you" to each other.

And then, and only then, could they begin to move on, to reclaim what they once had...if it even still existed.

Karl turned from the window and lay down on the futon. He closed his eyes, even though his heart was hammering, even though sweat poured from his hairline, his pits.

One way or another, this had to stop. It was not sustainable.

Chapter Six

"I want you to stop worrying about what happened in this apartment before we lived here, okay? I think you've gotten stuck in some kind of rut—a very disturbing rut. But you're not yourself." Ernie eyed me and the concern creasing his features made me ache.

He went on. "Everything's unpacked and you still have a few days more off. Blessed free time. Can you just do me a favor?"

I nodded, pretty sure I knew what was coming.

Ernie continued, "Today, I want you to reward yourself for all your hard work, for all you've done to make this place a home for us. Do something fun; go over to the Music Box and see a movie; have an afternoon cocktail at Roscoe's. Or maybe you could take a walk along the lakefront or ride your bike. It looks like it's going to be nice out today." Ernie gestured toward our windowed wall and he was right: unlike the day before, pure, undiluted early morning sunlight streamed in. Promising, falsely or not, warm breezes and boundless outdoor fun.

"Okay. You're right. You are absolutely right." I smiled and got up on tiptoe to kiss his full lips. He grabbed the back of my neck and thrust his tongue deep inside my mouth, kissing me hungrily and letting his hands wander down to my ass. He pulled away, a little breathless, and laughed. "That's to hold you until I get home from work. No bad dreams tonight. Just bad Ernie—maybe more than once. Hell, maybe more than twice!"

"Promises, promises." I gestured toward the door. "You better get a move on or you're gonna be late."

"Promise *me* you won't spend the day brooding about this Tommy and Karl. They've been weighing too heavily on you and I don't like it. We just moved here, for Christ's sake. This was supposed to be our *happy* home, not our haunted house."

The night before, after the L train dream, I had awakened screaming.

"I promise." I handed him the brown sack lunch I had packed for him, feeling every bit the housewife. "Now run along."

I felt bad. I didn't like to lie to Ernie.

He left and I listened at the door for his footfalls on the stairs, the slam of the vestibule and outer doors.

At the window, I watched his progress toward the L station. When he was out of view, I threw on some clothes and headed for Paula's.

*

When she opened the door, I could see she was dressed for work. She had pulled her frizz away from her face, almost severely, and had put on makeup—a ton of it: eyeliner and mascara, shadow, blush. Her lips were a glossy orange-red. She wore big dangling silver earrings, and her ensemble of a bulky black tunic top, tights, and heels actually made her look thinner. And all the makeup? In less talented hands, it might have been garish, but I was actually pleasantly surprised by how damn good she looked.

I almost didn't recognize her.

But of course I didn't tell her that. Instead, I said, "You look hot."

She reached out and pinched my cheek. "Thanks, babe." She left the door standing open as she bustled about the apartment, checking JoAnne's water bowl, hunting for her keys, finding them, and gathering up a big black leather satchel. She paused at her dresser to spritz come cologne behind her ears. The scent was spicy with no floral undertones. It suited her.

Turning to smile at me, she said, "Do you need something, hon? I have about five minutes before I need to head out. I'm one of those intolerable punctual folks, so I leave extra early because you know how the L can foil the most perfectly planned itineraries."

I felt guilty. I knew I was being selfish. Not only was I pretty sure I was about to make her late for work, I also would bet money on the fact that I was about to ruin her day. Part of me wished I could just leave things alone. But these appearances or dreams or whatever they were, weighed on me. The most overriding thing about them wasn't the fact that they were creepy (they were), but that I experienced a need coming from Tommy. He was trying desperately to get my attention. I didn't understand why he'd picked me, but it felt as true in my gut as anything I'd ever experienced.

I stepped into the apartment and closed the door. Her eyes flashed when I did that. Did I see a bit of fear? Annoyance?

"I saw him."

"What?"

"I saw him. Karl. Last night, I dreamed of him." I recited the images from my dream, told her about my nocturnal train ride that was both between the Irving Park and Addison Street stations and back in time.

Paula sat down at her table and lit a cigarette. "And you saw a foot on the bed?"

"Yeah. I bet it was Tommy's."

Paula considered this, and then shrugged. "What do you think it means?"

I had been waiting for the question, hoping she would ask it, so that the door would be opened to my theory. I sat down quickly across from her. "Listen, Paula. I don't want to hurt your feelings. I don't want to open old wounds. We just met and I'm aware I'm treading on what might be very painful territory for you." I paused and she nodded, looking longingly at her closed front door. I bet she was thinking if she had just gotten out of there five minutes sooner, she could have avoided all of this.

"Karl was crying, right?"

She nodded.

"I think he was crying because Tommy was dead."

Paula shook her head. "No, no. They never found a body. If something had happened, Karl would have called an ambulance, called the police, even if it was an overdose or something." She stared down at the table and when she looked back up at me, her tears had wrecked her careful makeup job. There were black streaks down her cheeks. "Karl would have told me; he would have told Tommy's family. You don't know them. Tommy's sister Amanda was a wreck. Is a wreck. She was older and loved that boy like he was her own son."

"I don't know what else to think." I blew out an exasperated sigh. "I don't get why this is happening to me. I certainly didn't ask for it. But I feel like there's a demand being put on me, this weird pressure. I honestly don't know if it'll leave me alone unless I deal with it. Does that make sense?"

"No. None of this make sense." Paula took a deep drag and inhaled the smoke almost angrily. "Oh shit, back at that time, when they were heavy into the drugs, it could have been a lot of things making him cry. They could have fought. Hell, I heard them screaming at each other and breaking things, especially when Miss Tina wasn't available. And I know Karl sometimes got jealous." She snuffed out her cigarette and placed her hand over mine. "Look, honey, I know you mean well, but leave this alone. I get that it might be hard—you seem like a sensitive soul." She stood. "Look. No one knows what happened to Tommy. My guess is he went off with one of the many, many guys he had over when he was usin'." She shrugged. "I gotta get to work."

She scooted her chair out from the table and hurried into the bathroom, where, I assume, she was repairing the damage her tears had done to her face. I called out, "Where's Karl?"

She stuck her head out of the bathroom. She had removed the lines of mascara that had dripped down her face and had a washcloth in her hand. "What do you wanna know for?"

Should I tell her why I wanted to know? Would she tell me where he was, once she knew I wanted to pay him a visit? I thought for a while, listening as she readied herself to leave for the second time that morning. Water ran; the toilet flushed. And I still couldn't think of a plausible reason why I wanted to see Karl, other than the truth.

Paula came back into the apartment proper and hoisted her big black bag over her shoulder. She was ready to go. "Really. Why do you want to know?"

I needed to tell her the truth. "I want to go see him."

She snorted. "Now, sir, that does not sound like a plan. It really does not. You have to understand. Karl's broken. It's been hard for him to get over losing Tommy and then what? You show up, a total stranger, asking your nutty questions, and it'll be like ripping a scab off a wound. You'll hurt him." She frowned and shook her head. "No, it's not a good idea, honey. You should leave this alone. If you just make the effort, I think these dreams or visions or whatever you want to call them will disappear with time. Get on with your own life—your job, your handsome man. Just let it go."

"I wish I could!" All of the sudden, I was on the verge of tears myself. "Please. Maybe if I could just talk to him, I could—" Even I didn't know where I was going with this.

"You could what?"

I paused, considering, trying to think with my head instead of my heart. Even I thought this was crazy. "I don't know. Maybe if we talked and I told him about my dreams, he would tell me if he knew something."

"Tell *you*?" Paula laughed and I had a glimpse of what an unkind Paula might be like. "Honey, he doesn't know *you*. Say your theory about him having an idea about Tommy's disappearance was true. Why the hell would he talk to *you* about it? Don't you think he's already been down this road a dozen times?"

She had a point.

Yet, I knew if I didn't get to the bottom of this, I wouldn't be able to find peace. In a weird sort of way, I was sure these dreams were Tommy reaching out to me. You can call me melodramatic or say I watch too much paranormal reality TV or too many horror movies, but something was nagging at me and not letting go. I felt as though our moving into that apartment had opened some sort of conduit. Why only with me, I had no idea, but there it was. But could I tell Paula any of this without her shooing me out of her apartment? I thought I could. After all, just a look around the place told me how much she believed in just the kinds of things I was thinking about.

"Look. You told me that you believed in an afterlife. You told me you thought there were things out there we couldn't conveniently explain away. Maybe my dreams are one of those things. Is it so farfetched? Look at it objectively, Paula. I didn't know Karl and Tommy, yet there they are in my dreams. How could that be?

"And those dreams are different from the usual garden variety I'm used to having. They have an odd sort of reality to them, more like they're memories or images of real events than dreams. They don't even feel like they come from me."

A ball formed in my throat, and my eyes welled with hot tears. I pressed the palms of my hands to my eyes to force tears away and took a few deep breaths to calm myself, to dissolve that lump lodged in my throat. I honestly couldn't pin down from where these emotions were coming either. I forced myself to breathe normally and smile. "I think Tommy is trying to tell me something. I think he's unhappy and something is unfinished."

Paula sat down heavily on her couch and stared at her hands.

I came to sit beside her. "Paula. You cared about him."

She looked up at me and nodded. "I sure did. My little Tommy," she whispered, her voice almost a squeak.

"Do you really think he just walked away? You said he had family here; you told me he had a sister he really loved—and she him. Don't you think, even if he was deep into drugs, he would have called someone? Just to let them know he's alive?"

Paula's lower lip trembled, and she drew herself up. I assumed she was looking for some of the same inner strength that I was. In a soft voice that was completely unlike her, she said, "When I say Tommy maybe ran off... When I say Tommy was a flake... When I say he just let the drugs get to him and he wasn't Tommy anymore, that's me, keeping a little door open. You know? A little door to hope."

She hung her head, and her shoulders shook; she sniffed. After a few moments, she allowed herself to look at me, but her eyes were red-rimmed. "Why did you have to come along with your dreams?"

She swallowed, and I suspected she had that same big ball of something burning in her throat as well. "I know. I know there must be something to it. You're right. Tommy wouldn't just have left and never been in touch again.

"But I don't think Karl had anything to do with it. I don't know what happened or why, but you don't know Karl. He's a sweetie; he'd never hurt his Tommy. He loved that boy! Even with all the drugs and the other guys, he never stopped loving him."

The two of us sat quietly for a long time. I listened as the trains rumbled by and the quality of the light changed in the room. I knew it was getting late in the morning and that Paula was too distressed to go to work. I had made her this way, but in an odd way, I didn't feel guilty about it. Some of this had to be a catharsis.

Paula stood and dug in her purse. She brought out her cell and punched in a number. "Keith? Hey, it's Paula. Listen, I got a bug or something, and I don't feel so hot, so I'm gonna stay home today." She paused. "Sure, I will. Bye."

She turned to me. "You really want to continue on with this? This whole mess doesn't have to mean anything to you. It's old news and nothing to do with you and that cute boyfriend of yours." She grinned. "Oh yeah, I've ogled him. I'm jealous." She held the phone up. "I can call Karl, or we can just try to forget this. If I call him, you realize you might be opening a door to something you can't shut, you know?"

I thought about my dreams and the nagging sensation that something outside myself was propelling me to action. The door was already open. And, finally, I thought Paula knew as well as I did that we needed to go on.

"Call him."

Before: The Good Times Are Killing Me

"It's been fun, hasn't it?" Karl was doing all he could to keep the sneer out of his voice, the sarcasm, and the pain. Of course, it had been fun the first couple of times. After that, it was simply what they called "chasing the dragon," the futile search for those early highs, the ones that made you feel invincible, that everything was right and exciting with the world. Karl, maybe, once imagined living in this golden world where nothing else mattered except the most incredible pleasure, one that exceeded his imagination and wildest dreams.

Except that world didn't exist. That world was nothing more than an empty promise. The world that *did* exist when one woke in the aftermath of a binge was dirty, scarred, a wound. Meth offered a promise that would be broken over and over again. Karl wondered why they weren't stupid enough to wake to the charade they were being fed by shards in a glassine bag.

Tommy stared out at him from underneath an old comforter, his beautiful eyes now rheumy and rimmed in red. He wore the blanket like a shroud, and Karl feared, after a few more encounters with the drug that had taken over their lives, that was exactly the result they might both end up with. Tommy's voice, now raspy and scarred from smoke, asked, "What the hell are you talking about?"

It was the opening Karl longed for, even if it wasn't exactly welcoming. He crossed the apartment, the hardwood gritty beneath his feet, to sit near Tommy. He knew that to sit too close would simply make him move away. There was also the fact that Tommy stunk to high heaven. Karl couldn't recall the last time he'd seen him take a shower.

But maybe all of that could end if he could get Tommy on board today, right now, with what Karl was about to propose.

"I spent the morning online, and I've found there are a ton of meetings we can go to, Tommy. One's even as close as a block away at the Episcopal church—it's a Narcotics Anonymous meeting and they meet this afternoon. We could go check it out."

Tommy eyed him, then smiled. But there was both wariness and weariness in that smile and something that looked to Karl very much like pity. "I don't need that shit. Those people are stupid—replacing one addiction for another." He chuckled and then coughed. "And the new addiction is a hell of a lot less fun."

Karl flopped back hard, frustrated, even though he knew in advance that Tommy would meet his plan with resistance.

Karl didn't know what to say. He'd had his own reckoning. If he was going to survive, he had to escape the siege crystal meth had taken on his life. He needed to do something. Twelve step groups offered a way out, even if they were only replacing one addiction with another, as Tommy had said. At least this new addiction offered wholesomeness and good health, perhaps a return to some semblance of a normal life. He embraced what he'd heard they said at the end of meetings with a fervent hope. "It works if you work it." For once, he felt a glimmer of optimism, of excitement. He wanted to try.

Maybe his—maybe their—future *could* change? Perhaps they could throw off their chains and be free? It was possible. Others had done it. There was no reason he and Tommy couldn't too.

After a long time, Karl responded to Tommy's dismissal. In a soft and what he hoped was a nonthreatening voice, he said, "The shit you don't need is Tina."

"I can—" Tommy didn't finish the sentence. His head hung.

"You can what? Quit anytime you want?" Karl shook his head. "Sweetheart, we both know that isn't true." Karl had lost time of the number of times they'd promised each other they'd quit. "You know as well as I do we can't do it alone. Maybe there was a time, early on, when we could, but that time is gone. We need help. Can't you see that?"

Tommy roused himself a little and glanced over at Karl. "You go if you want. I don't need to hang out with a bunch of pathetic losers. It won't make a bit of difference."

Karl closed his eyes and silently counted to ten. He could argue. He could say he and Tommy were the ones who were "pathetic losers," but he knew in his heart that such arguing would not advance his cause at all. Now, he wished he knew exactly what *would* advance his cause...

Oh, why did he care? He realized he couldn't force Tommy to have the same come-to-Jesus moment he had, but dammit, he loved the guy. He wanted them both to get sober, to get back on track, to move forward into a world where their lives weren't dominated by drugs.

A voice inside him, one very much like the voice he'd heard only a few days ago, after he'd come off a three-day binge and found himself alone in a filthy apartment, one that wasn't his own, with no idea how he'd gotten there or with whom he'd interacted, told him that, as ruthless as it seemed, he was in this alone. No one could do the hard work of getting sober for anyone else. As much as he loved Tommy, he couldn't save him.

Karl saw it like swimming to shore when you knew someone else was drowning. You could try to save that person but, in the process, could be pulled under yourself.

"Just come with me, Tommy. See what they have to say. You might be surprised. I'm not asking you to commit to anything. I'm not asking you to do anything other than sit beside me at an hour-long meeting. Is that too much to do…for me?" Karl felt his eyes well with tears. He took a stab in the dark. "I only ask, babe, because I love you so much."

Tommy stared straight ahead, and Karl had no idea if he was getting through or not.

After a while, Tommy gave him a one-word reply. "No."

Karl's shoulders sunk. He was too tired. The accumulation of their abuse for the past several months weighed on him—the sleepless nights, the ups and downs, the weight loss, the poor health—all of it came together to make him feel hopeless.

Almost.

He rose from the couch. "Okay. Let me know if you change your mind." He was going to leave it at that, thinking he was propping a door open so Tommy could follow, but then a dark cloud surrounded him and, still smiling, he said, very softly, "That shit's going to kill you. Or I will."

And then he headed toward the door. He'd find a coffee shop or a park to sit in until it was time to go to his first meeting.

Chapter Seven

The train screeched and rumbled as it hurtled us to the Western stop on the Brown Line—and maybe an uncertain future. Western was my former stop, my old neighborhood, just minutes away from my new one.

How odd that Karl and I had simply changed places. Perhaps our moving vans passed as we made our way to different lives.

Karl made it clear he didn't want to meet with us. I could tell as much from the one side of the phone conversation I overheard. Yet Paula pleaded with him, and she must have been persuasive enough. He didn't invite us to wherever he lived now. He *did* agree to meet us at the Starbucks on Lincoln and Wilson. Paula told me, after hanging up, that he said he only had a half hour or so; and then he had to get to work.

I laughed as we got off the train, not because anything was funny, but simply because I was suddenly so nervous. A week ago, if someone had told me I'd find myself enmeshed in such bizarre circumstances, I would have told that person they were crazy. And yes, I get the irony—maybe I was the one who was crazy. Still, we were here.

Soon, we'd be meeting a major player who'd figured in my nightmares.

Paula glanced back. "What's so funny?"

"Oh God, nothing. Actually—*this*. This whole situation. I never would have believed I'd be doing this a week ago." I felt like I'd suddenly taken the lead role in a movie, only I knew none of my lines, nor what character I was supposed to be playing. It was a master class in improvisation.

The train lurched to a stop and the door slid open. We joined the other passengers disembarking. A wind blew toward us from the north, chilling. We headed down the stairs and out of the station. A train rumbled on the tracks above us. This used to be my old stop. It felt so familiar. I'd come out of this train station countless times before.

We headed south.

"What's he like?" I asked.

"Karl?" Paula shrugged. "He's a nice guy. Not as crazy as Tommy was..." She stopped herself when I think she realized she referred to Tommy in the past tense. "Not as crazy as Tommy, but sweet. He's worked hard to rebuild after Tommy left."

Even though the day was bright and sunny, there was still that snap of cold in the air. We headed down Lincoln Avenue, the traffic heading north and south. It seemed like just another ordinary day. And at the same time, I felt like I was on a precipice, at the edge of *anything could happen.*

It felt good once we got inside the Starbucks, warm, the place redolent with the smell of fresh ground coffee and scalded milk. There were a few folks at the tables with their laptops and their smartphones, engaged. A few more swarmed around the counter, awaiting their orders.

We stood near the door, looking for Karl.

What if he doesn't show up? He doesn't have to. Lord knows this situation is weird enough. Based on what I knew of his sad history, I could understand why he might change his mind and want to steer as far clear of the guy living in his old apartment as possible. I couldn't blame him.

But if he didn't show up, where would it leave me? I didn't see anywhere I could go from here without Karl's help.

I'd have a relentlessly nagging hole in my psyche with no way to fill it, that's where I'd find myself. I didn't know if I could bear it. This was something that, somehow, had to get settled.

Paula said, "There's Karl." And I looked to where she had nodded.

He sat at a table near the back of the café, his head down over a cup of something. He clung to it, as if it was keeping him warm. Anyone else, waiting for someone, would be looking up, alert for their arrival. But Karl seemed to want to vanish into the steam wafting up toward his face.

I had expected to see a man in the same sad shape that Tommy was in, the ravages of crystal meth addiction apparent on his body and face, but that wasn't the case. Karl looked like he had in the photo Paula had shown me—vital, alive, his streaked hair perhaps a little darker and more uniform, and perhaps even a bit stockier. The signs were there that he had left his old pal Tina behind.

And that was good.

We approached the table and he grinned when he saw Paula. But when his eyes fell upon me, he frowned. He stood and he and Paula exchanged pleasantries and hugged. She scolded him for not being in touch more often. When Paula introduced Karl to me, I reached out to shake his hand.

The touch of his hand was electric. Very quickly, I had an image of him dragging a long, sheet-wrapped bundle. And then the image vanished before I could place it in any sort of context. Still, it shook me up.

"Nice to meet you," Karl said.

"You too." I looked around, needing a moment away. I didn't know how ready I was to talk. "Listen, I'm gonna get myself a latte. Paula, what do you want? And Karl, can I get you some more of whatever you've got there?"

Paula ordered a plain drip coffee, black, and Karl said he was fine.

When I returned to the table, both Karl and Paula were quiet. Paula stared at the other people in the coffee shop—an older woman with a laptop, and a group of kids playing hooky from high school, I would guess. Karl continued to look morosely down into his cup.

I realized it was going to be difficult to broach the subject we had come here to talk about. I could see the discomfort on Paula's face as she sipped. From my limited knowledge of her, she was usually brassy, loud-mouthed, and talkative. This withdrawn, quiet state was completely out of character. It was almost as though she'd morphed into a different person—shy and reticent.

I could see it would be up to me to lead this meeting. I was torn between wanting to get started and simply smiling and then turning to run out the door.

My eyes met Karl's. We stared at one another for a long moment and I felt some sort of connection. I wish I could describe it, put into words what it meant, but I was clueless. I only knew that I felt something strange, something electric, when I stared into his eyes. I almost wanted to say, "You know, don't you?" But I censored myself, thinking just how loony that would sound.

He drew his gaze away first. His voice was cold. "Is there a purpose to this meeting, Paula? Some of us have to get to work." He glanced over at me. The look was not kind. "I don't know who this joker is, but I'm not in the market for any new guy in my life if that's what you're about." He took a breath and a sip of his coffee. "And the fact that he lives in my old place, well, that's supposed to mean *what* to me?"

Should I just come out with it? How can I tell him about the dreams without him thinking I was a nut case? And if he did have something to do with Tommy's disappearance, was this meeting opening a door to danger?

I drank my latte, not tasting it, and wishing I had thought this through more before we got on the train to come over here. But yet, even as Paula was dialing Karl's number, I had felt something outside myself was propelling me. It was almost as if I had no choice.

Paula broke the silence. "Rick here, as you know, lives in your old place. And—it's the weirdest thing—ever since he and his boyfriend Ernie moved in, he's had these odd dreams."

"So?" Karl no longer met my eyes.

"They're about you and Tommy." She turned to me. "Why don't you tell him about them, Rick?"

I froze. For several moments, I felt as though I couldn't speak. Again, I had that sensation of being in a movie or on stage and having no clue what lines I was supposed to utter.

Karl returned his gaze to me, scowling. And finally, it was he who spoke, not me. "I don't want to hear it." He stood. "This was a mistake. I knew it would be. I don't know what this is about, but it doesn't interest me. I have no interest in a trip down fucking memory lane." He looked toward me. "And whatever your game is, fella, I can assure you, I have no interest in getting involved."

Paula gestured toward his seat. "Sit back down, honey. You work from home, for cryin' out loud. There's no time clock to punch." Paula tried to placate him.

Karl was having none of it. He got up from the table so quickly his coffee cup overturned and a pool of milky brown liquid began to widen on the table before us. Paula scooted back quickly to protect her clothes, blotting at the puddle with the paper napkins I had brought back to the table. "Jesus!" she cried. She called after Karl's departing figure, "Karl! Karl, come back here. We just want to talk to you, sweetie!"

Everyone else went quiet, staring at us. Heat rose to my face as I watched Karl exit the café. In seconds, though, the storm passed and everyone went back to what they were doing before Karl rushed out.

"I don't know what to say." Paula continued to blot up the spilled coffee. "He's usually not like that. Karl was always the nice one; the one who couldn't even hang up on a telemarketer."

Again, I felt this almost irresistible pull to do a thing I wouldn't normally do. "I have to go after him." I half rose out of my seat.

"Oh, honey, I don't think you should." She reached out to grab my hand with her own. "What do you think it will get you?" She finished mopping up Karl's mess and then slid the pile of sopping napkins to the side. "You should leave this alone," she said softly. "Really."

I shook my head. Leaving Karl alone, for me, simply wasn't an option. "I have to go after him."

And suddenly, nothing seemed more imperative.

I left Paula sitting slack-jawed at the table and hurried out of Starbucks.

Before: Watching

Tommy had followed Karl the whole way to his Narcotics Anonymous meeting at the neighborhood Episcopal church. It had been easy. Karl was so preoccupied with where he was headed, Tommy guessed, that he never sensed someone was behind him.

And now, Tommy stood across the street from the Atonement Church in the shadows at the side of a redbrick three-flat apartment building.

Tommy couldn't help but notice the irony of the name. The church was nothing fancy—a newer white-brick building with stained glass windows and big double glass door in front.

The people attending the meeting, as far as Tommy knew, were not Episcopalians. Karl himself always said he was a "lapsed Catholic in need of a good spanking." But there he was, standing near if not exactly with, the dozen or so other people waiting for the meeting to begin. Karl and one other woman, with a streak of magenta in her blonde hair, were the only ones not smoking as if their lives depended on it.

Tommy felt dead inside, but he'd made himself follow Karl because he thought, maybe, just maybe, he might surprise him and join him at the meeting. He didn't know what he'd do or say, but he felt like it was the least he could do, given the anguish he witnessed on Karl's face when Tommy had refused to go to the meeting with him. Part of his refusal was steeped in his belief that Tommy was too far gone in this dance with addiction. He didn't know what it could take to pull him back from the edge of the abyss, but he doubted it would be sitting in a room full of contrite strangers, spouting out the misery they felt at being ensnared in a web they'd woven themselves.

The other part of the reason he'd managed the Herculean task of getting off the couch, dressing, and following Karl when he was crashing hard was that he'd believed, that if he'd refuse Karl on the plan to attend the meeting, Karl wouldn't go. Up until the moment Karl walked out the door of their apartment, Tommy believed he'd come right back. He'd join him on the couch. There were still a few little crumbs left in a Baggie on the bedroom nightstand, and they could fire that up in the pipe, put on some porn, and get back to what now passed for normal for them.

There were few things Tommy could count on anymore, but Karl getting high with him was always one of them.

Except when it was no longer the case.

Karl had surprised him. Tommy was sure he was bluffing. Oh yeah, they might attend the meeting together if Tommy had deigned to go along, but all they would do was roll their eyes at one another at the pathetic losers on display, telling their sad tales of misspent lives. And then they would come home and get high.

But this time had been different. Karl had actually left him alone in his misery on the couch.

Karl looked scared. Tommy could see that even from across the street. He made no attempt to join in any conversations. He stood with his hands thrust into his jeans pockets, staring down. It was as though he wanted to make himself unapproachable. Maybe there was still hope, Tommy thought. He tried to telepathically send a message to Karl, *Come to me. I'm right here. Let's go home. Be together. You don't need this.*

But it appeared his transmitting was a dismal failure. He watched, still unnoticed by Karl or anyone else, as the doors at the back of the church opened and people took one last drag, exchanged a few final words, and began milling inside.

Karl was the last one left outside, and despite the distance of the two-lane street separating them, Tommy could see the indecision on his face.

Go to him. Go the meeting. As Karl said, all you have to do is sit beside him and listen. Nothing ventured, nothing gained. In spite of this train of thought, Tommy stayed rooted to where he was.

And he almost let out a small cry when Karl joined the others and went inside.

It's not too late. Cross the street. Go. Tommy shook his head. What good would it do? Did he really want the boredom and monotony of getting clean and sober?

The little Baggie on the nightstand called to Tommy, called louder than Karl could.

He knew just a little hit on the pipe would revive him, erase this deadness in him that made him feel he weighed a couple of tons.

Tina was always there for him, even if that bastard Karl was not.

Tommy, safe from prying eyes now, emerged out of the shadows and started to make the soul-sucking and exhausting walk home—all two blocks of it.

The walk home seemed to take forever. Tommy was tired, down to his very bones. He had to stop during the short journey a couple of times, just to rest against the side of a building. If it didn't look so weird, perhaps eliciting the concern of passersby, he would have simply slid down to the ground, legs stretched out before him.

But he persevered, continuing onward, until he got home.

Halfway up the inner stairs, he had to sit down. Sweat was cascading down his face. His chest was tight and his heart within pounded so hard Tommy feared it would explode, leaping right out of his chest. He gulped air and his breath came in short, desperate pants, like a dog on a hot summer's day.

A shadow fell across his shoulders. Oh no. I don't need to see anyone right now. I don't know if I have even the energy to speak.

"Tommy?"

It was their neighbor Paula. Tommy hung his head.

He could hear as well as feel her padding down the stairs in bare feet. She stood now just behind him on the step. "Tommy? Hon, are you okay?"

He turned to gaze up at her. With the window behind her, she was nothing more than a broad, bland silhouette. "I'm good," he croaked.

She was leaning over him, enveloping him in some woodsy scent that almost made him puke. "No, you're not." She groped under his armpits, lifting.

Breathlessly, he got to his feet, shrugging her off. At last, the light was right—he could see her face. "Really, Paula. Just got a little winded is all."

"Winded?" She squinched her eyes up, confused. "You're what? Twentysomething? And *this* winds you?" She shook her head, her bright eyes alive with concern.

"Yes," was all he could manage to say. He tried to edge by her.

"Let me help you, sweetie."

He moved away. "Get away from me, bitch." He felt bad, talking to her that way. But this was the last thing he needed right now.

"Tommy," she whined.

He didn't look back. He simply forced himself to put one foot in front of the other and somehow, hard as it was, he mounted the remaining stairs. He could feel Paula watching him all the while. She was probably too scared of him to utter another word. Or maybe too pissed.

He didn't care. He leaned against his apartment door, mortified that he'd left it unlocked. He got inside and leaned against the door to shut it behind himself. Listening for Paula's footfalls coming down the hall—but there was nothing. Like Karl, he thought, she's given up on me too.

Well, I don't give a flying fuck.

He found the Baggie and moaned when he saw it was empty. There was only a little white dust inside. He tore it open and licked the bitter remnants.

*

Tommy gripped the phone in his hand so tightly his knuckles whitened. His hand hurt. He wanted to cry—not a few tears, but wah-wah-wah, like a cranky baby overdue for a nap or a bottle. *Oh well, it's the same kind of need, right?*

He'd told Sam, the dealer they'd dealt with from the very start of this whole sordid journey he needed to buy a teener, or a sixteenth of an ounce. He wanted an eight-ball, but a teener would have to work, because it was all he could afford.

He expected to run through the same routine as always. Sam, mock-friendly, would ask, "What you need?"

Tommy would tell him, and like Dominoes, Sam would deliver, usually within a half hour or so. He'd glide to the curb in his black BMW and text Tommy to come down.

Tommy would. He'd slip inside the spotless car, exchange the very minimum of small talk, and then they'd surreptitiously make the trade of cash for drugs.

If only everything in life could be so simple, fast, and easy!

But this time was different.

Sam's Turkish-accented English was tense. "Can't do it, man. Sorry."

"What can't you do? Deliver? I can meet you somewhere." Tommy felt himself getting a little breathless. He needed his stuff *now*. Whatever it took...

"That's not it, buddy."

"What the fuck? What do you mean?"

Sam sighed. "Look, I did you a courtesy answering your call. Your boyfriend, Karl, was in touch with me." He paused for a moment. "He said you guys had a problem with the stuff and needed a break. He asked me not to sell him or you any more. Normally, I wouldn't do that, because I'm a business guy. But Karl seemed really scared. You know? Like your using had gone beyond recreational. He said you, particularly, had a problem."

Sam went silent after that.

"Karl doesn't speak for me."

"Uh, yeah. In this case, he does. Listen, I have lots to do tonight, so I'm gonna hang up."

"No!" Tommy almost screamed. He tried to take it down a couple of notches. "No, Sam, please wait. Listen, I'm okay. Karl and I..." His voice trailed off. He and Karl were what? Tommy didn't know. "Karl doesn't know what he's talking about. I'm fine, just fine."

"You're not."

"Look, how can I convince you?"

"You can't. Now, I need to go."

"Listen, man, I'll scrape up the funds and pay you double what I normally do. I just need a taste."

Sam blew out a big sigh and Tommy was really afraid he'd make good on his threat to hang up. And then where would he be? What if Sam blocked his number? Sam said, "It's not about money."

"I could blow you too." Tommy shook his head. He wasn't so far gone that his face didn't heat up with shame. Sam had never given him any indication that he would be receptive to such a thing.

"Dude, you're pathetic." Tommy heard him light a cigarette and exhale. "And I'm straight."

"Just this once. And then I leave you alone. I promise."

The silence went on so long that Tommy's next word was, "Hello?"

"I shouldn't do this. One last time, man. And then that's it. No more. I block you from my phone. You call. I don't get it. Okay?"

"Sure, sure." Tommy was shaking with need. At this point, he would have agreed to anything.

"I shouldn't do this. You could have a heart attack. Or a stroke. You think you're too young? Think again."

"You're right, man. You're right. I won't bother you again." Even Tommy knew himself for a liar. Sam blocked him? He'd find someone else.

Or maybe he'd join Karl at the next NA meeting.

Who knew? Who cared? All Tommy knew was that right now, he had an awful itch and Sam would help him scratch it.

What was it Karl had said to him right before he set off for his meeting? "That stuff will kill you. Or I will."

*

Sam steered the BMW north on Lake Shore Drive. The lake was to his right and, peripherally, he could see the white-capped waves crashing against the shore. He thought he shouldn't be doing this. He didn't need the pittance Tommy Soldano would place into his hand in crumpled, dirty currency. He had dozens more in line for his product. There was never a shortage of buyers.

And that made Sam sad. Made him question just what the hell he was doing with his life. He'd never been tempted, as he knew some dealers were, to use his own stuff. Not even once. Because if there was one thing Sam knew, it was that one time was never enough. Not with this shit.

That's exactly why this was such a lucrative business.

So, Sam kept away. His only vice was the half a pack of Marlboro Reds he smoked every day. And even that vice, he thought, chuckling to himself, was in danger. His wife, Azra, was forever after him to quit. With the birth of their little boy, Freddie, he knew she was right.

He'd quit tomorrow.

Maybe.

He exited at Irving Park Road, thinking about the call he'd had only yesterday from Tommy's boyfriend, Karl, pleading with him not to sell them any more meth. "It's bad, man, for both of us. If we call, just ignore us. We can get clean if you do. We don't know anyone else to get it from. Not really."

The poor guy had started crying. And so Sam had agreed. He knew it wasn't his place. His place was to act as a supplier. That was it. If folks got hooked, that was their problem, right?

Yet Sam knew, in his heart of hearts, what role he played in the drama of addiction.

Maybe he'd quit more than cigarettes in the future. There were better ways to make a living. He'd make a lot less, but he could work in his father's discount furniture store on Devon Avenue.

But at least he wouldn't be harming people.

Maybe even killing them.

Anyway, this would for sure be the last delivery he'd make to Mr. Tommy Soldano. He pulled out his phone and shot Tommy a quick text letting him know he was here, even though Sam would swear he could feel Tommy's gaze on him as he pulled up.

As he waited in the idling car, he brought up his contacts in his phone, found Tommy's number, and blocked him.

What happened to Tommy after today was out of Sam's hands.

Chapter Eight

Once outside, I thought I had lost Karl. There were too many people on Lincoln Avenue. Swarms of them, human camouflage. Not one of them looked like Karl, though. Or maybe *all* of them looked like Karl, and I was left with the riddle of finding the real man among the clones.

I turned and looked north, where the L tracks made a kind of bridge over the street, and didn't see him among the throngs pouring in and out of the station. I peered south, where I could see downtown's buildings in the distance, but no Karl. I hurried to the corner and leveled my gaze east on Wilson Avenue.

And that's when I spotted him.

He was rapidly heading east, casting looks every few minutes or so behind him. Probably worried that I had taken it upon myself to do the very thing I was doing. It didn't take him long to spot me. He stopped in his tracks and even from the distance of half a block or so, I could tell he blew out a frustrated sigh. He crossed his arms and stood facing me, not moving, his legs planted wide apart. As I drew closer, it was clear that his features had contorted into a snarl.

I hurried to catch up, smiling in a way I just knew looked foolish, but I couldn't help myself. My smile was my only defense, so I figured I might as well work it as best I could.

When I reached him, I blurted out, "I'm sorry, but we have to talk."

His reply was almost a scream, high-pitched and tortured. His tone and reaction told me a lot. "I don't want to." His eyes had the look of a trapped animal as he regarded me. "Why can't you just leave me alone? I can't help you, man."

Despite his words, he didn't turn away. I could take that inaction as a small victory.

I reached out to put a placating hand on his shoulder as a bus roared by, but he shrugged it away. I leaned in close and talked in as soft and reasonable a voice as I could muster. "I know you don't want to talk. But you know we have to."

"Why do I know that?" He eyed me impatiently. "I don't know any such thing, except you're some fucking nutcase."

"But you *do* know, Karl. I could tell by the way you looked at me back at Starbucks. You know something, and it's eating you alive. You'll feel better if you just get it out. I'm not here to judge or make you afraid."

And then it came to me, unbidden, yet clear and unquestionable. I don't know how I knew it, but I was more certain than I'd been about anything. I eyed him and said, "You've been having dreams too."

The look on his face, the shock and fear, confirmed everything.

"I don't know what you're talking about." The words were a lie. He knew it as well as I did.

"Yes, you do," I said calmly. "You know because it's true. Come on, it's just us now. There's no reason to pretend otherwise." *Please, please, please, I need to unburden myself of this mess. I need to get free.* And I believed, deep down, that somehow Tommy needed my help. And this was my only course to giving it.

Karl's face twitched, and he looked all around, as if his savior might be hiding somewhere nearby, right here on Wilson Avenue. He shook his head, and I wasn't sure at all I was going to get anywhere with him. But I had to try.

"You live near here, right?"

He sighed. "Yes. But you're not coming over, if that's what you're thinking."

"Would you rather we talked about Tommy's death right here on the street? Or his murder?" An old woman passed us—very conveniently—at just that moment. She turned to look at us, and I was sure Karl also caught her stare. She continued on down the street, dragging her shopping cart behind her, casting suspicious glances every few steps.

"I'd rather not talk about Tommy's death at all. You don't know me. You know nothing about me."

There was raw pain on his face. His skin paled a few shades lighter, and it was as though someone had extinguished the light in his gray eyes. I think we both realized he had said "Tommy's death" and what that meant. He didn't say "Tommy's disappearance." He said death. I didn't believe it was a simple slip of the tongue.

"I know you wouldn't. Who would choose to talk about something so painful? And I can't blame you. But I have been having these dreams."

"I know," Karl whispered. He stared down at the ground and finally admitted, in a voice scarcely above a whisper, "I think I've been having the same ones."

"And they just started this week?"

Karl nodded. His face had gone completely white.

"Tommy's still around. We both know it." I forced Karl to meet my gaze. "Something needs to get settled."

Karl said nothing for the longest time as we stood there, two men who barely knew each other, watching as the traffic passed by, going east, going west. At last, he let out a sigh and told me, "I live over on Damen."

And he turned and started walking rapidly. He knew I'd keep up.

His apartment was a little studio on the third floor of a redbrick building at the corner of Damen and Eastwood, across from a gas station. The apartment was almost obsessively tidy, with the bed made up, the kitchen sink and counters empty and wiped clean and not so much as a magazine or coffee cup out of place. There were no pictures on the walls, no framed photos graced the top of a bookshelf or a desk. The only decoration in the place was an orchid in a pot that was doing quite well and a sampler above Karl's computer desk. The cross-stitched words were the time-honored ones: *one day at a time.*

Karl sat down on the edge of his bed and did not invite me to join him. He grabbed a throw pillow to his chest and stared out the window. Other than a pure blue sky and the very tip of the gas station's sign, I could not imagine there was much to see.

I surprised him and sat on the bed next to him. I did not, though, try to touch him.

It crossed my mind then that I could be sitting next to a killer, a killer with a secret he wanted to keep hidden. Often, at least in the psychological suspense and true crime novels I devoured on my L train rides to and from work, that alone was enough motivation to kill again.

I took a nervous swallow and said something that might have seemed strange, but I thought it would at least let him know we were not as alone as he might think. "Paula may be right behind us, so we should make this quick."

"I don't know what you want from me."

"How about the truth?"

Karl didn't say anything for a long time. Long enough that I was beginning to think he was stonewalling me, and silence would be his escape. If he didn't say anything, simply didn't open his mouth, what could I do? It wasn't as though I could pry a confession out of him with my fingers.

"Karl?" I said softly.

It was as though he had been waiting for this moment. I couldn't have dreamed that his release would come this easily. But I suppose when you've kept something pent up as long as he had, maybe there was some relief mixed in with the anguish.

But I'm getting ahead of myself here.

I jumped when Karl let out a long, anguished sob and began crying, his face in his hands. Not knowing what to do, I patted his back and let him cry.

Another series of long moments passed when I began to wonder if this would go anywhere other than a grief session.

He pulled himself together and lay back on the bed, which was positioned next to the window. He stared outside and said, "Tell me about your dreams."

I slid to the floor, so that I was leaning against the bed with my legs stretched out in front of me. I had an instinctive sense that this conversation would be easier if we were not looking at each another. We were, after all, only strangers brought together by extraordinary, maybe even otherworldly, experience.

I told him about the dreams, about seeing Tommy with his pipe, his desperate call to his dealer. I let Karl know I had seen him standing near the bed, wracked with grief. His anguish had been apparent to me even in the dark, even from the distance of viewing it from a train car for only a moment or two. I didn't mention, though, the vision I'd had from the L tracks, where I could see Karl standing at the end of the bed, the white foot just barely in view.

Karl sobbed in the background, softly, sniffling.

I paused then, debating whether I should tell him about the quick vision I had had of him dragging the sheet-wrapped bundle. It could force his hand. It could also perhaps make me another sheet-wrapped corpse.

The vision had come to me when we shook hands in Starbucks. If I told him that, it would let him know that I thought there was a good chance he was a murderer. I honestly didn't know how safe I would be. I shivered and eyed the door, wondering how quickly I could get up, cross the room, and fling it open if I needed to.

Again, we were strangers in a quiet room, discussing the most intimate of stories.

Why would he have done it? I mean, why does anyone kill the person he or she professes to love? Had it been in a fit of jealous rage? Was he trying to get away from the drugs and Tommy refused to accompany him on the journey? Was it the other way around?

I wouldn't know anything unless I spoke up. I would have to trust that this big, furry man on the bed beside me was as gentle as he seemed.

"You dream funny." I heard Karl sit up behind me.

"What do you mean?"

"It's like you plucked the memories right out of my head. Or out of Tommy's." And then he said something that further confirmed everything. And even though I had suspected it, his next words chilled me to the core. "God rest his soul."

"So." I had to summon up the courage and the strength to ask what I wanted to know, the question, really, that had been with me all along.

"So, Tommy *is* dead, then?"

Like Paula—and in spite of my dreams and the odd case of the washed plate—I held out some hope that this was a weird misunderstanding and that Tommy was still alive, working out his problems in some rehab facility in Florida, or living in a halfway house with other addicts. Or, worse, that he was still caught up in the throes of his addiction and perhaps was nearby, but was too ashamed and too enmeshed in his own personal nightmare to be in touch with the people he loved.

Karl wiped all of that out. "Yes. Tommy's dead."

Silence fell upon the room once more, again for so long that I wondered if anyone would ever speak again. But Karl finally said, "There's no doubt about that." The words tumbled out haltingly with a catch in his breath. Even though I couldn't see his face, I knew the man was struggling mightily to hold it together.

The question slipped from between my lips like a pent-up thing, like something with a mind of its own. "Did you kill him?"

Karl didn't answer right away. I began to think a guilty person would pause; an innocent one would denounce his culpability immediately. "In a way, I guess I did. But not how you think."

I turned to look at him. He was lying on his side on the bed, facing me. There wasn't much expression on his face; I suppose I would describe him as a man about to jump off a cliff.

"Tell me."

He did.

Before: A Dream

Silence. Save for the tick of a clock, there's no other sound.

"Please, Tom, eat something." Karl sat at the foot of the bed, balancing a white melamine tray on his knees. On it was a rapidly-cooling mug of tea, Earl Grey, Tommy's favorite. Karl added three teaspoons of sugar and a generous splash of real cream. There was a chipped Fiestaware plate, cobalt blue, and it contained two slices of white bread, lightly toasted. Karl had even peeled an orange for him, removing seeds and pith, cutting it into wedges.

"I can't. You know I can't." Tommy turned away from him in bed, making the flatware and dishes rattle on the tray.

Karl sighed. Tommy knew this was an uphill battle for him and, if he had any awareness at all, one he could never win.

Tommy stared at the wall, waiting for the sound of Karl rising, walking away, footsteps down the stairs, to the kitchen, where he will patiently dump the tea and throw the toast into the trashcan.

He'd done it a thousand times already.

And all the while, Tommy withered away. The last time he was able to stand on the bathroom scale, he gasped at what it revealed. He was officially below one-hundred pounds, the first time in more than a decade. Tommy had taken one last look at himself in the bathroom mirror and wanted to scream. His ribs showed. His skin, ashen, gray, clung to his skeletal frame in folds.

He knew he needed to eat, but the very idea of it caused his stomach to churn sickeningly. If he could bring anything at all up, he would have.

So he lay here, drifting in and out of consciousness. There was only one thing that could possibly make him feel better, and Karl refused to get it for him.

How much longer?

Tommy's eyelids fluttered and he felt his waking state slipping away again. He surrendered because it brought him oblivion, as a little Baggie filled with shards once had.

Silence. Save for the tick of a clock, there's no other sound.

Tommy's alone and doesn't know where he is because it's too dark to tell. He could be in the middle of a desert or shrouded deep in a forest. All he knows is that he's by himself. He wanders through the darkness and the silence, the air hot on his skin.

His face is slick with sweat. The perspiration is crawly, like an insect's legs, as it trickles down his spine. The earth beneath his feet is coarse, sandy.

Above him, the sky is an endless dome of black. No stars, but every once in a while, an explosion. A burst of orange and red above, fire.

He smells sulfur.

He opens his mouth to scream, but no sound emerges. All that happens is he sucks in hot air, and that makes it even harder to breathe.

He'd run if he could, but his legs are heavy, weighted to the ground as though there's metal in his feet and magnets in the earth.

Silence. And the clock tick, tick, ticks off the minutes.

And then the ticking stops.

Another flare of orange and then a whiteness so bright it blinds him.

He can scream.

When he woke, Karl stood at the foot of the bed. "You were screaming," he said.

The room was dark, lit only by an L train rumbling by. Tommy attempted to sit up, but it was too much for him. The few inches he'd lifted his head off the mattress were futile and he slumped back down.

Karl moved around to the side of the bed. He set a glass of water and a couple Tylenol in a saucer on the nightstand.

"Mama," Tommy whispered. He managed a snicker.

Karl tenderly lifted Tommy's head and folded the pillow beneath it so Tommy wouldn't choke when he swallowed. He stooped to take up the water and the pills. "Down the hatch. Okay, sweetie?"

Tommy just shook his head. "Sleep," is all he managed to say. He croaked out a few more words, "I can finally sleep."

Karl standing over him, his face awash with concern, was the last thing he saw imprinted on the backs of his eyelids as he dropped again into oblivion.

The light of the L, in the distance, rushed closer.

And Tommy felt himself rising toward the stamped-tin ceiling. He looked down upon himself, lying on the dirty, sweat-stained sheets. Karl was beside him, head hung, distraught.

He stopped and tumbled back down to the bed. *Too soon, too soon...*

Chapter Nine

"It's not like you think. I didn't lay a hand on him. I didn't strangle him. Or shoot him. Or stab him. Or put a pillow over his face.

"I didn't kill him directly. But I might as well have.

"See, I was the one who introduced Tommy to a lady known as Tina. You know who she is. You can't be gay in this town without coming across her. She's fun at first, but then she goes quickly from being fun—once she has her claws in you—to being a demanding bitch, stripping everything out of your life but her.

"I brought her home to Tommy. At first, we snorted a forty dollar bag, which now wouldn't even be enough to raise my heart rate, but for us, it was magic. This was about two years ago.

"It's amazing how fast things can go downhill!

"We just did it on the weekends to start. And it was doable—we'd get high, watch some porn, have mind-blowing sex that lasted for hours, as long as we had a little Viagra in the house. Miss Tina is murder on an erection, you know? They call it 'crystal dick' for a reason. She gives you this insatiable desire, and then takes away the means to do anything about it. Yeah, we found out quickly enough how a bit of Tina and one of those little blue pills went hand in hand. A match made in heaven.

"Or hell.

"Like I said, it was just on the weekends at first and just us. Then we started toying with the idea of having another guy over. We'd go online on Adam4Adam or something like that and look at the pictures of other guys and talk dirty about what we'd do with them. It was like the porn; it got us revved up even more, and we'd end up in bed, or on the floor, but always behind our little screen. You know the one? We left it there for you. I couldn't take it when I moved. It represented too much ugliness, too much pain. But going to the hook-up sites? We both thought it was just part of our fantasy, nothing more.

"But it didn't take long before the porn, talking dirty, and looking at sex ads online wasn't enough. We had somebody over, and after he left, we both felt sheepish and guilty and promised we'd never do *that* again." Karl stopped for a minute, remembering. "And then we broke down and there was somebody else, and then another one. And then a couple of guys. It just got easier and easier. Somewhere along the way one of those guys introduced us to smoking the stuff, even left behind his little glass pipe, and that just escalated things for some reason. The smoke got into our system faster.

"In nothing flat, we were having guys over all the time. Safe sex flew out the window. Sex with each other flew out the window. We just wanted more and more dick, and it seemed like no matter how much we got, it was never enough. The question was always, 'Who's next?'

"We both came up poz. It didn't stop us. It didn't even slow us down. We told each other it was a relief. We didn't have to worry anymore about becoming poz. There was other stuff too. Charming. We got herpes, the clap, MRSA...it didn't stop us. It didn't stop us because too much was never enough.

"And we started needing more and more Tina to just feel normal. It didn't really make us high like it used to, but when we were without, it was hell. We'd fight, hurt each other—we became a regular George and Martha.

"I think, deep down, we knew we still loved each other, and it was the drug that was making us act as we did. I mean, we both changed when we were under the influence. Completely. Different people. Selfish people. People who had no standards. You should have seen some of the creeps we played with.

"Oh and doing it only on the weekends? That went by the wayside real fast. It started out with doing little maintenance bumps in the morning, then taking some to work with us, and then finally when we were getting up— if we'd even slept the night before—smoking up and calling in sick.

"Then we'd party and play all day.

"We both got real skinny and, looking back, I know we both appeared so sad and sickly it was a wonder anyone would have anything to do with us, but they did." Karl laughed, but there was no mirth in it. "I saw this meme once somewhere, and it was a picture of a guy on his hands and knees getting plowed from behind by, wait for it, E-fucking-T. The caption was something like, "When you party with Tina, you'll let anyone fuck you." He shook his head. "Funny 'cause it's true. All us tweakers were caught up in the same cycle. It didn't matter, really, what anyone looked like, as long as they had a dick and party favors.

"Everybody we came in contact with were just like us. If we had favors to share, I suspect we could have been six-eyed monsters, and they wouldn't have cared.

"Pretty soon, Tommy lost his job, and I was just barely holding on to mine. We got behind in everything—rent, utilities. We spent money that should have gone for food on drugs, but that was easy because we never wanted to eat. We borrowed against credit cards, maxing those out.

"I hit bottom one night when I was sitting on the toilet, bleeding from my ass, while the fucker who made me bleed was giving the same deal to Tommy.

"That was ugly. I felt sick. Worried. And the guy I loved was in the other room, getting banged by some stranger we'd probably never see again. And neither of them could have cared less about me. Nobody came to check on me. I was out of the room and, consequently, didn't matter.

"I wanted to stop using, desperately, but Tommy didn't. He just became consumed.

"Finally, it *did* consume him...like a monster just eating him up. One night, when I came home from work, I found him barely able to move on the bed. I tried taking care of him, I really did. By this point, I was in the process of getting clean myself. I thought if I set an example, led the way, my Tommy would get on board. Anyway, I did what you do when you have a sick loved one in the house—I made soup; I made tea. It was like trying to stop a tsunami with a garbage can lid." Karl hung his head in shame.

"I know I should have done more than just what I did. I know it. I should have taken him to the ER. This wasn't just crashing after a binge. The poor guy could barely move. His skin was cold and clammy. He was talking shit. Paranoid shit. There were listening devices in the walls. He could hear whispering in the hallway just outside our front door. Laughter. He thought the mailman was a DEA agent, ready to barge in with a whole crew, like you see on that old TV show, *Cops*."

Karl closed his eyes, as if the memories were too much, as if they were eating him alive, which I suspected they were. I didn't think he could go on, and I leaned in to place a hand, some comfort, on his forearm, but he yanked away as though my touch had the power to wound.

Maybe it did.

He drew in a shaky breath, holding back tears. This had to be painful. Was I the first person he'd revealed these details to? If so, this unburdening must have been akin to lancing a wound, offering both relief and the deepest horror.

The room grew darker as we spoke, the very world reflecting, with waning light and heavy clouds, Karl's confession—a cosmic mirror.

He surprised me, though. I suspected he wouldn't want to say any more, would want me to leave, yet he went on. "I left him alone for a while, thinking some sleep would be good for him. I was going to go to sleep myself, after staying up late channel surfing. I went up to the loft to check on him, to beg him once again to eat a few crackers or take a sip of tea." Karl's lower lip quivered, but he pulled himself together.

"That's when I found him dead on our bed." The words hung in the air between us, the coda to the story I already knew. But Karl saying the words out loud made everything real.

He eyed me, trying, I suppose, to gauge my reaction. "It was just like you saw in your dream or whatever. I'm sure Miss Tina just squeezed too hard on his overworked heart. Or maybe she short-circuited his brain. It should have been dramatic, but it wasn't. Death's prosaic. Bland. Like taking a dump. There was nothing over the top about Tommy slipping away." Karl shook his head. A tear ran down his cheek.

"It was sad. That's all. He had turned white, his ribs stuck out, and vomit coated his chin and lips.

"I didn't know what to do. I wasn't thinking clearly. I thought I'd get blamed. Charged with murder. We were notorious druggies. Paranoia was my constant companion." Karl stood and looked down at me. His emotions did a change, going from despair to rage. "It was stupid. So fucking stupid! But I decided in the heat of the moment. Nothing would bring Tommy back. And him dying could very well ruin my life."

A cold chill ran up and down my spine, as though some icy living creature had penetrated my skin and was now running amok.

"Don't blame me, okay? There wasn't a damn thing I could do to revive him, you know? He had no pulse. He wasn't breathing. Believe me, I checked. I also did mouth-to-mouth. Chest compressions. But dead is dead, right? Once someone's gone, they're gone."

Karl crossed the room to stare out the window. He didn't look at me as he said, "So I made him disappear. I cleaned him up and wrapped him in sheets and waited until about 4:00 a.m., then I took our sad little Ford Fiesta, pulled it up to the front of the building and put Tommy in the hatch. Even at dead weight, he felt like nothing.

"I took him out to a forest preserve off Golf Road in Des Plaines. I went into the woods with my Tommy and a shovel. I dug for hours. It was muddy, wet, and the hole kept filling with water, but I got it good and deep—I didn't want some animal digging my Tommy up, and I put him in.

"I covered him up and I knelt down by his grave and scattered a pile of old leaves and twigs overtop it.

"I was sure the whole time I'd be caught.

"But I never was, as you know.

"I said a little prayer for him. Tommy had this book? He'd held on to it from when he was a little boy, an altar boy at St. Aloysius back in his hometown. Oddly, it was on the nightstand the night he passed away. I'm still not sure how it get there. Maybe he knew he was going to pass and put it there. Anyway, it was called *Little Folded Hands*. I brought it with me to the forest preserve. When he was all tucked into the earth, I read it over him. Wanna hear it?"

I nodded.

Karl's voice, broken, as though he'd swallowed broken glass, emerged in starts and fits, but he got it all out.

"Now the light has gone away;
Savior, listen while I pray.
Asking Thee to watch and keep
And to send me quiet sleep.

Jesus, Savior, wash away
All that has been wrong to-day;
Help me every day to be
Good and gentle, more like Thee.

Let my near and dear ones be
Always near and dear to Thee.
O bring me and all I love
To Thy happy home above.
Amen."

"I ended with promising Tommy I'd never do that shit again." He turned away from the window to look at me, sitting spellbound on the bed.

"And I haven't. Haven't even touched a drop of alcohol, let alone drugs of any kind.

"So you see, I *did* kill Tommy in my own way. And not giving his family or people who loved him like Paula any closure, I know, was a very bad thing to do.

"But the question is—what do we do now? And what do I do with you? Now that you know..."

Karl came toward me. I recoiled.

Before: Unveiling

Karl hadn't found the book, *Little Folded Hands*, on the nightstand. That was a lie. Who knows why he told it that way? It did make for a mysterious edge to his story, but the truth was he found it, along with a bunch of Tommy's belongings, in a cardboard printer paper box under their bed after he returned home from burying him.

The idea was to clean the place up, remove from it all traces of Tommy. Karl could say he'd taken off, run away, left in the night. The story would have more credence if all of his meager possessions were gone.

Karl had already loaded up a couple of garbage bags with Tommy's clothes, a few books, and some CDs. It was sad—to come to the end of a life and all Tommy's worldly goods fit in a couple of trash bags. Garbage. No one would miss it.

Karl choked back a sob as he wondered if anyone would really miss Tommy himself. The drug, in its short trajectory, had already removed Tommy's presence from the real world, the humdrum everyday that we call life.

He was almost finished when he noticed the printer paper box under the bed. He supposed it had been there the whole time, amid the dust bunnies and flip-flops, but it was just one of those things that had never elicited any curiosity from Karl.

He pulled it out and took off the cover. On top was a can of butane, a torch, and a couple of glass pipes, the meth residue black at the bottom of their bowls. Karl shook his head. "Oh, Tommy, Tommy, Tommy." He took the paraphernalia out and put it in one of the garbage bags, sinking it deep among the clothes so the pipes wouldn't break and puncture the bag.

But beneath the crap that had killed him were signposts to a different Tommy—a clean, wholesome young man in his prime. Karl remembered that person and felt numb. He'd already cried his eyes dry. But his hands shook as he looked at the old school photographs, the edition of *Gay Chicago* he'd saved because on page 37, in the "Out and About Town" section, there was a picture of the two of them together at Sidetrack on what was their one-year anniversary. They both looked fit, maybe even a little chubby, their smiles indicating their happiness at just being out, being with the other. There was an employee manual for Tommy's job downtown. There was a Cyndi Lauper cassette—her greatest hits. There was a rubber-banded stack of letters. Karl could see from the one on top, they were printed-out emails they'd written to each other, both before and after they met. Karl couldn't bear to reread them.

And then, there it was—at the bottom of the box. Something unexpected. Karl pulled out the few yellowed pages carefully as though they were fragile, delicate paper that would turn to dust, even though they were only a few years old.

His eyes welled with tears as he gazed down at the application Tommy must have filled out right about the time they were moving into the apartment where he would one day draw his last breath.

The application was for an accelerated program to become certified to teach in Chicago area schools. One needed a bachelor's degree to apply, but little else. Once accepted into the program, coursework and student teaching could be accomplished within a year or maybe a bit more.

And it all came back—how Tommy had told him once he'd wanted to teach high school English. "I think I could really throw a genuine love for literature into these kids just by picking out some cool stuff for them to read—William Golding, James Baldwin, JD Salinger, Joyce Carol Oates. Good writers, you know? But still, on the most basic level, entertaining storytellers."

In his mind's eye, he had perfect recollection of that conversation, even though it hadn't swum to the surface of his conscious mind in forever. He could see Tommy's bright, clear eyes, his winning smile.

His hope.

Karl had never known he'd filled out this application. Hell, he'd never even realized such a program existed and that Tommy was interested.

It was so sad. Maybe he'd been about to mail this in when Karl had brought home that damned little glassine bag with its shards and its false promise.

He put the application back and shut the lid on the box. He began the process of taking things out to the car. He could get rid of this stuff in the dumpsters behind the Jewel on Broadway.

It was as though Tommy had never existed.

Karl shook his head.

Tommy would always exist in Karl's heart. No matter what, he'd always be with him.

Chapter Ten

Karl had told his story with a curious lack of passion. And his last question, the one directed at me, chilled me to the bone. "What do I do with you?"

I turned to look at him once more and he simply stared at me, with little expression. The room had darkened almost completely as he spoke, and it added to the dread I felt. I leaned over and switched on a floor lamp, but all it did was add an isolated pool of sickly yellowish light to the room, hardly illuminating.

I was afraid.

Sure, Karl seemed sad, remorseful. But he was a guy who'd buried his lover in a forest preserve. Why hadn't he simply called the police? Called Paula, next door? Called Tommy's sister, Amanda? There were any number of things he could have done beyond such extreme—and illegal—measures.

How could he have left Tommy's friends and family wondering? In the dark? With no closure?

It was cruel. I couldn't imagine if one of my family members, or even Ernie, just vanished off the planet with no explanation one day. Would I ever get over the loss?

Could I ever stop wondering where they were, if they'd show up again one day? Was hope an extinguishable thing?

Should I try to stand and walk quickly to the door? Did I have anything on my person with which I could defend myself if he tried to, um, *silence* me? Phrases such as "leave no witnesses" and "dead men tell no tales" ran through my head, almost making me erupt in giddy, near-hysterical laughter.

He must have noticed my fear. Or maybe he smelled it seeping from my pores.

He gave me a sad smile and shook his head. "I'm not going to hurt you, if that's what you're thinking. I couldn't hurt a bug, let alone a full-grown human being. It's not in my nature." He sighed. "I know I said I killed Tommy, but I didn't do it directly. I couldn't have. I loved that man with all my heart." Tears stood poised in the corners of his eyes. "Still, if not for me, if not for me introducing him to something toxic, he might be alive today."

Part of me wanted to reach out and hold him, or at least lay a comforting hand on his shoulder. But another part held back. Of course, I didn't believe he'd actually killed Tommy, even if he had introduced him to the drug that eventually did.

Tommy was a grown man; he bore some responsibility for his own death. He didn't have to take the drug Karl offered. He didn't have to continue using. He could have sought help, as Karl had.

But something else rankled me, ate away at me. I thought of my own family, my mom and dad, my brother Greg, his wife. They'd be sick if *I* just disappeared. Their grief and sleepless nights invaded me in a way that surprised me. I shook my head, trying to clear it of an image of my mother in a dark room waiting by a phone that might never ring.

And then I thought again of what I would be like if Ernie simply didn't come home from work tonight—and didn't come home the next day, and the next, until I simply never saw him again. What kind of life would that be? Would not knowing be worse than knowing he was dead? I didn't know, but I would think, in order for me to move on, it would be better if I knew *something* no matter how bad. It would ruin my life more than if Ernie broke up with me or even died.

"We have to tell people. You need to go to the police." I said the words softly. I was afraid to put the conviction I felt in my heart behind them. I didn't know this man sitting behind me on his bed. I didn't know what kind of argument I was in for.

Yes, hope would be gone, but at least I'd know. And with that knowledge, I could perhaps begin to make peace with tragedy. I could find solace in memories and maybe even move on.

Karl had taken away that option.

Dusk was upon us. Even in the twilight outside, I could glimpse gray, low-hanging clouds that promised some kind of precipitation before too long. Was it too early for snow? *This is Chicago. It's never too early, or too late, for snow.*

Karl finally spoke. "We can't do that. I'll go to jail. Who would that help? I mean, seriously. I'd do it in a heartbeat if it would bring my Tommy back. I'd die for him, you know."

I turned to look at him. "Is that all you can think about? Yourself?"

His features contorted into anguish. "It's not that. I mean, telling isn't going to bring him back, not really. And I *will* go to jail, no doubt about it. And it might be easy for you to minimize, since you're not the one who would be put behind bars, but it *is* a consideration." He sighed. "I don't know that I'm ready to martyr myself that way."

I didn't know what the penalty was for covering up a death, or worse, for burying a body in a public forest preserve. Accessory after the fact, maybe? I began to think I should just walk quietly out of here and once I got a few paces away from the building, call the police on my cell. But I didn't have enough to tell them. Sure, I could accuse Karl, but he could just deny what I said; what proof was there? My dreams? It would be a simple case of my word against his. And I bet he realized that.

I couldn't lead them to a body, for god's sake. In the Chicago area, the forest preserves had to number in the thousands and thousands of acres.

And yet I felt I had to convince Karl, somehow, to do the right thing. "No, no, of course it won't bring him back. He's gone and nothing can change that. You seem like you've tried to make some sort of decent life for yourself, like you've managed to get yourself clean."

He snorted, but it was a bitter laugh. "When you hit the bottom like I did, it's easier than you might think. There's suddenly nowhere to go but up."

I went on, realizing that Tommy's hand was guiding me to this moment, tasking me with revealing his fate and his whereabouts.

"You know Tommy's family. You know Paula. You know their grief, their anguish. It has to be horrible—not knowing. It's like a nightmare, only they can never wake from it. You must realize that if they had some idea of what happened to him, it might give them closure. It would hurt them, sure, and they *would* be in horrible pain. But that's the thing—they haven't been permitted *to grieve*. Not when they're in this sort of ignorant limbo. You could release them. Don't you want to do that?"

I didn't say it, but I thought it. *Tommy's in limbo too. As long as his passing is a secret, as long as he can never be properly mourned by the people who loved him, he's stuck between here and whatever the afterlife is. Oh, Karl, let him go. He's begging for it.*

"Of course I do!" Karl wailed, his voice shrill. "But is it really so selfish of me to not want to compound everything that happened with me being put behind bars? Yes, I know how selfish that sounds, but I just can't see what good it would do." He circled around to his original argument again. "It wouldn't bring him back."

Then I thought I should voice what I'd been thinking. He'd opened the door. "But maybe it would make him go away."

"What?"

"I told you about my dreams. And you know better than anyone those aren't just dreams. Hell, they don't even come from my own mind. They're Tommy. And Tommy is not at peace. He latched on to me like some kind of psychic savior and not only made me see what I saw, but compelled me here to be with you in this room. I'm sure of it."

Karl took a long time before he said, "I am too." He hung his head, which gave me a small measure of relief. Was I beginning to get through?

"Do you have a picture of him?" I asked.

Karl got up from the bed and went to his dresser. He opened the top drawer and rummaged around, finally pulling out a greeting card. It was a Valentine, a big kitschy Hallmark affair with a huge red heart and glitter. A snapshot dropped out. Karl held it out to me. "Here, this is all I have now."

I took it and looked down. It was a picture of Tommy in bed. Don't get the wrong idea, though. It wasn't provocative pose. This must have been taken on Christmas morning. Tommy was sitting up, shirtless, with one of those stick-on bows on his head. Whatever gift he had just gotten was hidden in a box on his lap, amidst the detritus of bright red and green wrapping paper. He smiled at the person taking the picture, who I had a strong suspicion was Karl.

There was pure joy on his face. Love in his eyes. Those qualities practically radiated off the matte paper upon which the photograph was printed. The photo might as well have been titled, "Before the fall."

Oh god! He was healthy—virtually glowing with vitality and vigor. There was no doubt in my mind that this had to have been before the drug invaded their lives, way before things began dissembling.

I handed the photo back to Karl. There was nothing much to say other than "He looks so happy."

"He was. It was our first Christmas together. He introduced me to calamari and baccala on Christmas Eve. Pizzelles and giuggiulena."

He put the picture down.

"Karl, Karl." I cocked my head. "How can you do this to him? Don't you see? *He can't rest.* He's all alone somewhere, both in the real world and some other place, somewhere none of us has ventured. None of us living, anyway."

Karl covered his face with his hands. His shoulders shook as he sobbed. I let him be, allowing him to ride out the storm of grief. After a time, he removed his hands and revealed red eyes and a face slick with tears. "Why did you have to come along? I wasn't happy, but I was letting it go."

"Really? Were you? All I see when I look at you is a miserable man. *I* didn't just happen to come along. Don't you see, Karl? It's not me; it's *Tommy* who's come along." I paused. "It's *Tommy* who wants peace. And I don't think he can find it when his death is a secret." I shook my head. "Not when his loved ones are in the dark as much as he is."

I didn't know if there was a lot more I could say. I stood up and stared out the window. Sleety rain, like needles, had begun to pelt the glass, smearing it and obscuring the view of Damen Avenue below and the lines of traffic going north and south, their headlights glowing like insect eyes.

I could feel Karl watching me, waiting for me to leave. I turned to regard him. He lay back down on the bed and closed his eyes, which I thought could reasonably be interpreted as a gesture of dismissal.

But then he spoke. "Tommy once told me that he never wanted to be alone. He was an extrovert, you know? He fed off other people, not in a bad way, like a parasite.

He just got energy—happiness—from other people. Me? I could go a long time on my own. I enjoyed seeing a movie by myself or having lunch out with only a magazine or a good book for company. Tommy couldn't understand that. He couldn't see the point of doing something if you had no one to do it with."

I got what Karl was saying. "He's alone now, Karl. That's maybe the most tragic thing, especially when you know how much he hated it. I don't know what's on the other side, but I like to believe all those stories we hear—about going toward the light, loved ones waiting for us—are true. And why can't they be?"

The bed creaked and groaned as I sat next to him. I raised my hand to indicate the view. "Look out there. The cold. The drizzle." I sat with him for a moment, both of us watching as the cold rain, almost ice, smeared the glass. "He's all by himself."

I paused for a moment, letting that sink in. "Listen, I don't really want to have to go to the cops with this; I'm not even sure I can. Cops need stuff like evidence to go on, a little thing like proof. So, you *could* lie. Tell them I'm crazy, which my boyfriend would probably back you up on." I laughed self-consciously.

"I have no real evidence. But I think you know what's right."

Karl sniffled a couple times and sat up. "Yeah, I do."

"What are you gonna do?"

"I don't know."

An idea had been brewing in the back of my mind. It was far from perfect and not entirely free from risk, but maybe it could work. And if it achieved the result of

Tommy's loved ones finally getting some closure, and Tommy himself some peace, maybe it would be worth it.

I took Karl's hand in my own. "How about this? What if I went out there, found one of those rare pay phones and made an anonymous call to the police?" Just the thought of actually doing this gave me a chill and caused butterflies to rise and take wing in my gut. It made me want to forget the whole thing, but then, as I've said, I was being pushed to do something. "You tell me, as best you can, where Tommy is buried, and I'll relay that information to the proper authorities. Can you do that? Give me some signposts to where they can, um, dig? They can take it from there."

"But, but—"

I held up a hand to stop him. I was pretty sure I knew what he was going to say. "Of course, I know there's a risk you could be caught. You lived with him; you have a big connection to him. They're going to look at you first. There may be some tough questions."

I sighed, my heart sinking. Maybe this wasn't going to work after all. "And who knows what evidence you might have left behind in that grave? Fibers. A bit of skin." I'd read enough true crime to know how damning the smallest piece of evidence could be, especially with DNA. I squeezed Karl's hand. "But it's a chance we have to take. It's the only way your man is going to find peace. It's the only way to end his awful solitude. Are you willing to take that risk?"

"If I'm not, then what happens?"

The answer came to me without deliberation. "Then I will go to the police and I will tell them everything I know. Your word against mine, I know, but I think just what you told me here today is enough of a red flag to raise some serious investigation." Even as I said the words, I wasn't 100 percent certain I could follow through, not with the thin evidence I had, which amounted to almost nothing. And if I couldn't give them at least some guidance toward where Tommy might be buried, I'd be just another nutcase, some true-crime theorist.

But Karl didn't call me on it. "I just wondered what you would do." He blew out a big sigh. "I already made up my mind, Rick. Let's go with your plan—the anonymous call. It's the right thing to do...for Tommy." He grabbed me and hugged me then, which stunned me. When he pulled away, renewed tears glistened in his eyes. "Thank you. You don't know how long this has been weighing on me. No matter what happens now, this feels like some kind of relief."

I stood. All sorts of emotions and beliefs coursed through me all at once—relief, sadness, a peculiar kind of joy. All of these were married to a weird sense of the surreal. Last week, I hadn't even known Karl, or Paula, or, especially, Tommy. Life was, yes, mundane. The supernatural entered into only when Ernie deigned to watch a scary movie with me. Yet here I was at the center of all their lives.

Tommy? I called to him in my mind. *Tommy? Can you hear me? This is for you.*

I moved toward the door. Now that I'd set things in motion, it was important to follow through, before Karl changed his mind. "I should go make that call. Do you want to give me some guidance on where Tommy is? Some landmarks? I think there's a pay phone at the Western L station. There used to be, anyway." I could see it in my mind's eye from back when we lived over this way. But pay phones? They'd pretty much vanished from the urban landscape. I had another idea. "If I can't find a pay phone, I won't give up." Inspiration came to me suddenly, borne of necessity. "If I can't find one, I'll swing by Walgreens and buy a cheap pay-as-you-go." Again, in my mind's eye, I could see the array of those phones behind the cashier, along with charging cords, batteries, cigarettes, and inexpensive earbuds.

Karl stood. He moved toward me, shaking his head. "No. This isn't right. Even though you got involved in our story in some weird way, you shouldn't have to make that call. It's not your responsibility. I'll make the call anonymously. Plus, I can make sure they know where he is. And then it will be over." He turned away and his shoulders heaved with sudden tears.

I squeezed his shoulder. I could feel him wiping at his eyes and heard him sniffle, pulling himself together. He turned to me. "You know what's weird?"

"What?"

"I think part of the reason—and I just realized this—I was afraid to tell was that it kept me, and me alone, connected to Tommy. Isn't that terrible? It was our little secret, something only he and I shared. That is, until he started 'talking' to you." He shook his head. "You must think I'm an awful person."

But I didn't. I understood.

Loving someone so much you can't let them go? Hey, once you love deeply and completely that's something with which anyone can empathize. "I don't. You're a good person who's done bad things. Just like everyone else." I opened the door and stopped, the light from the hallway filtering in.

"Now, I'm leaving here believing and trusting that you're going to make that call. That you'll help Tommy and everyone else who loves him say a proper goodbye. I can count on you, right?" I didn't want to threaten him and the peace I felt inside, the first all this week, told me he wouldn't let me down.

"I'm going to go do it right now." His lip trembled a little and in the dim light, I could see he had gone pale. "No matter what, I'll do it. For Tommy. Promise."

"Good. You take care." I stared at him.

We were strangers once more.

I hurried out the door.

Chapter Eleven

It was only two days later when Paula showed up at my door. It was a Saturday morning and Ernie had gone down to Ann Sather to take care of his craving for cinnamon rolls and coffee. He planned to bring a box home. I was doing a little cleaning and had the stereo turned up loud to distract me from wiping down surfaces. *Madonna's Greatest Hits*. Ernie would have been mortified. He was a traditional jazz kind of guy. He thought Madge was a cultural abomination who'd long ago worn out her welcome.

Anyway, I digress.

The knock startled me. I put down the rag in my hand and then shut off the music. I hurried to answer the door.

Paula stood in the hallway, looking kind of shell-shocked. Her lower lip trembled a bit, and her hair was in disarray. She wore only a pink chenille bathrobe that made me think of my mother. I didn't tell her that. We faced one another across the threshold, and it seemed as though Paula was struggling to speak.

Ernie knew very little of what had gone on. I hadn't related the details of my visit with Karl. I believed the fewer people who knew what had actually happened right here in our home, the better. It made more sense that way. I debated whether to ask her to come in or suggest we move to her place. I glanced behind me before closing the door. "Do you mind if we talk over at your place? Ernie will be home soon, and I don't wanna get interrupted."

From the look on her face and that morning's *Chicago Tribune* in her hand, I knew what was on her mind. The news had leaked out late last night—it wasn't a big story, but enough of a mystery that it made the paper.

Once she closed her front door behind me, she handed me the newspaper. "You know about this?" Her voice just barely held it together, skirting grief, barely avoiding sobs.

I set the newspaper back down, folded open to the story about the body of a man discovered in the forest preserve in Des Plaines. "Yeah. I saw it in the online edition early this morning. I'm so sorry, Paula."

She plopped down at her messy kitchen table, littered with a half-drunk cup of coffee, a plate with a partially eaten Pop Tart on it, and the other sections of the newspaper. Paula groped her way through the mess until she found her cigarettes. With a shaking hand, she lit one, blew out the smoke and regarded me. "I still can't believe it. I mean, the practical part of me knew, deep down, that Tommy was dead. But as long as there was no proof, there was still that little smidgen of hope. I clung to that sucker." She smiled, but it was one of the saddest smiles I'd ever seen.

"This makes it real, you know?" She shook her head, looking down at the news item, which told the story I now knew by heart. It told of the anonymous tip, the discovery of the body in a heavily wooded area of a suburban

Chicago forest preserve, and the identification of that badly decomposed body as one Thomas Soldano, who had been reported missing more than a year ago. Identification was made using dental records. Foul play was suspected.

Only I—and Karl—knew just how foul. Not very foul at all, not really. Just sad.

I wondered how much Paula knew.

I wondered how long it would be until detectives showed up at Karl's door. The sad truth was he would be their prime suspect. And from the mental state I'd observed him in, I was pretty sure it wouldn't take him long to break down and tell the truth about what had actually happened. He didn't kill anyone and maybe he could get them to believe that. But covering up a death? Burying a body on public property? Things wouldn't, couldn't, go well for him. When the truth finally came out, and I was positive it would, Karl would be looking at some jail time. Maybe not life in prison. But he'd spend a few years behind bars.

"Yeah, I know. I get it. But at least now the truth is out." I put my hand over hers, gave it a squeeze, and then returned my hand to my lap. "How you holdin' up, hon?"

"I'm okay. In some ways better and some ways worse than before I knew, for the reasons I already gave you." She eyed me. "Have you had any more dreams?"

And that was the thing—I had not.

No dreams about Tommy since Karl and I came to our agreement and this morning's reporting from the *Chicago Tribune* verified that Karl was a man of his word. My slumber had been calm and, as far as I could recall, the only dream I had had was Ernie and me in some dark room, with Ernie bending me over a table. Hardly what anyone would refer to as "haunting."

"No. I haven't seen a thing." I thought I would feel unburdened and free after a night of no visitations, or dreams, or whatever the hell had plagued me. But the truth was, I missed Tommy. I missed the excitement. I missed the puzzle. Life would now return to normal, or what passed for it. And that was a sobering prospect. But this wasn't about me, so I said, "I think it was what he wanted. Tommy, I mean."

"I know you're right." She shook her head. "I can't imagine who would have done such a thing to him. I'm still trying to get up my nerve to call Karl. That's gonna be a tough call. He's gonna be devastated." Her eyes took on a faraway cast, and I knew she was imagining her poor friend, beyond her suspicion, being broken by the news. She lit a second cigarette off the butt of the last and blew the smoke toward the ceiling. "Ah, who am I trying to kid? It's news now. He probably knows already." Tears stood in her eyes, but they didn't fall. "He's with Amanda, Tommy's sis, right now and they're comforting each other." At last, the tears fell, and she smiled. "Who am I? Just the nosy next-door neighbor. Why should they involve me?"

"Oh Paula, you were their friend. You cared. Maybe later, you should go over and see Karl, let him know he can count on you." What was I saying? I knew how Karl's call, anonymous or not, had to be nothing more than a house of cards. For all I knew, he'd already been picked up by the police.

So she knew nothing and didn't appear to suspect Karl. Of course she wouldn't. One thing was obvious—

Paula had loved the guys. Had mourned them both even before they were gone, as they sunk into the quagmire of addiction.

I certainly would never tell her what I knew.

As Karl had wondered aloud, what good would it do? It would only hurt Paula more to know what he'd done. Even though I doubted it, I hoped Karl got away with it. And maybe he would—with little more to go on than an anonymous tip, the authorities might not think it was worth their while to chase this down. Chicago's ugly side was that it was a city filled with crime, murder, gangs. A drug addict's body, missing for more than a year, wouldn't be a priority. "I'm sure. I can't imagine. But I also think he probably feels a little better now that everything has been brought to light."

"I don't know. It's a hard thing. Those boys loved each other like nobody's business. Having Tommy found like this is going to just reopen all that pain for him."

"But at least he'll know, and he can start to heal." *As can Tommy*, I thought, but didn't say.

"Yeah. We all can." She stubbed out her cigarette. A pall of blue-gray smoke hung near the ceiling, and it was starting to make me feel claustrophobic.

"I talked to Tommy's sister, Amanda, and they're planning a memorial service for him. Wanna come with me?"

I was surprised to hear this. I had just assumed Paula had been alone with the sad news and that I was the first person she'd come to with it.

I needed to let this go. I'd done what I thought needed to be done, played my part. "That's awfully nice of you to ask, Paula, but I'll pass. I don't really know those people, didn't really know Tommy, although I think we had a connection." My thoughts, like my words, trailed off. "I don't belong there." My admission was the truth, but it made me feel oddly sad, nonetheless. I'd been so absorbed in solving the mystery of my nocturnal visitor that I'd forged a kind of connection with him. Shit. Even I was now mourning his passing.

It was all such a waste. In addition to the visitations from Tommy, I knew that this toxic mix of chemicals had snuffed out a life, even before his heart stopped beating. Meth had stolen Tommy's youth, his will, and most of all, his hope. He should never have died so young, not as he did.

His death, really, was avoidable. It was just a matter of never picking up a pipe or just putting it down. But something—how he was wired, maybe—had made that impossible, even at the cost of his own life.

Paula and I sat in silence for a while. We were once again people who barely knew one another sitting across a messy kitchen table. What connected me to Paula had been broken and I wondered what would happen now. Would we be friends? Hanging out like she used to with Tommy and Karl—cocktails at Big Chicks, in and out of each other's apartments? Or would the memory of those two phantom men always haunt her with Ernie and me serving only as painful reminders? Or would we simply be cordial neighbors, making small talk when we passed in the hall?

I didn't know. I did know, though, that whatever happened between us, it couldn't be forced. It would grow on its own, organically. Or not.

But I did know whatever we became, it would be something different from what she had with Tommy and Karl.

I walked over to the front door and put my hand on the knob. "Ernie's getting us Ann Sather cinnamon rolls, and he'll be back soon. I should get back." I smiled, but she didn't see because she was staring out the window, far, far away. "I could maybe bring you one later."

"That would be nice," she said softly, not looking at me.

"Take care, Paula. We'll talk soon, okay?"

"Sure thing, hon."

I turned and walked out the door, leaving Paula alone to do some long-overdue mourning.

*

I awakened to darkness and the gentle tap of rain on our big window, the window that had attracted me to this strange and unique apartment. I lay still in the darkness, listening to Ernie's even breathing beside me and thinking about when I had first noticed the place we now lived in.

Had it been around the time Tommy had passed away? Had he been leading me here from the start?

I turned away from Ernie and pulled the sheet up tight around my ears. I was just about to close my eyes when I noticed the other bed, just beside my own.

Tommy was on it. He was naked and his body looked pale in the darkness, skeletal. He was wrapping a belt around his arm, looping it and pulling it taut with his teeth. He tapped the skin, searching, I suppose, for a vein. I could see the hypodermic needle lying on the stained sheets next to him.

"Don't do it," I whispered, reaching out a hand toward him.

But he picked up the needle, worked it into a vein, and plunged it home. I cringed as he immediately began convulsing, only the whites of his eyes showing, his back arched.

His head flopped to one side and a dribble of vomit bubbled out of his mouth.

And then Tommy was still.

I sucked in a breath and tried to swallow around a lump that had formed in my throat. So this was how it happened, then? No drama, just sad and pathetic. One more victim.

But as I watched, another Tommy rose above the dead thing on the bed. This Tommy seemed to be crafted from otherworldly light, glowing. He was healthy, robust, his body lean and packed with muscle. His eyes sparkled and when he turned to look at me, he smiled.

He was free.

Our front door opened. There was the clatter of feet on the stairs. And then an anguished voice I recognized as Karl's cried out, "Tommy! No!"

Even Ernie stirred at Karl's cry. "Hmm? What was that?" His hand gripped my shoulder.

I turned to him. The images vanished, like wisps of smoke on the air. "Nothing. Go back to sleep." Ernie complied, no arguments.

I rolled over so that he and I were spooning and pulled Ernie's arm around me. In a few seconds, he was snoring. The extra bed and Tommy and Karl had all been swallowed up by the darkness.

An L train rumbled by outside, its light confirming that there was no one here but Ernie and me.

I knew Tommy wouldn't be back.

As I said, he was free.

After: Rick

Three weeks had passed since Tommy's body had been unearthed in the forest preserve, based on information provided in a very detailed and credible anonymous tip. I imagined it all when I read about it online, although the details were sparse. But I have imagination to spare, so I visualized a white canvas awning pitched to protect the gravesite, bright lights on tripods illuminating the rain that would have been inevitably pouring down. Forensic technicians scurried around the site, measuring, snapping photographs, calling out discoveries.

I didn't dare imagine Tommy himself, lying in the damp earth in an old sheet, his skeleton a kind of sad souvenir of a young life, badly lived.

The unearthing wasn't exactly front page news. Sad, but it appeared only in the online edition of the *Trib*. There were no accompanying pictures and only the briefest of descriptions. It hurt me to realize how little Tommy's life mattered to anyone beyond his immediate circle.

It had been two weeks since Tommy was laid to rest, beside his mother and father at Rosehill Cemetery on the North Side of the city. I thought about going to the funeral, since I'd invested so much energy into getting Tommy the peace of this final resting place, with its old mausoleums, historic monuments, and a lovely pond where geese and swans congregate. But I would have felt like the intruder I was. I had a specific role to play in this tragedy and it was done.

The last three weeks of my life had been oddly anticlimactic, for which I was grateful, I guess. I'd be a liar if I said I didn't miss the drama and excitement and, yes, even the terror of what had played out in our home.

But a return to being simply yet another gay man living with his boyfriend in Chicago was welcome. Sometimes, it's nice to blend into the crowd. In the past three weeks, Ernie and I had settled into the apartment, trying to make it our own.

We got rid of the lurid screen by carrying it outside and placing it beside a dumpster in the alley behind our building. I checked, maybe having second thoughts, about an hour later. It was gone. That was probably for the best because I knew how many secrets it hid. Anyway, it was never ours to begin with. It was a painful reminder of a life lived in a kind of manic pain, and who needs that? Whoever found it in the alley would have no idea of its history and that was for the best.

We painted the kitchen cabinets a cobalt blue color and bought new handles and pulls in pewter. We headed out to Schaumburg and, at Ikea, bought an assortment of new rugs to soften the effect of the scuffed and weary wooden floors. I was all about bright primary colors to add cheer to the depressing, almost-winter skies already closing in.

Settled. We picked up on our previous life and started getting together with friends for nights out at Giordano's Pizza or a foreign film at the Music Box or comedy night at Sidetracks. As time went by, I even had a day or two when I didn't think about my strange encounters with Tommy Soldano and, in the real world, his boyfriend, Karl.

One Saturday morning in early November, I looked outside and saw clear blue skies with only a few strands of clouds, like cotton candy, up high. Even though the weather app on my phone told me it was only in the high forties (and not expected to go much higher than that), I yearned to get outside. I wanted the feel of relatively fresh air and sunlight caressing my skin.

I took the steps up to the loft two at a time and dressed in a pair of sweats, a long-sleeved T-shirt and a pair of Brooks running shoes. I wanted to simply walk along the shores of Lake Michigan, to take in the smell of the water and how the sunlight would dapple it with diamond-like sparkles. I wanted to savor the view of the city's skyline to the south, mingle with the guys fishing from the breakwater at Hollywood Beach.

From the way the trees were bending outside, there was a healthy wind and that bode well for big waves. I could already feel the spray from them on my face as I headed downstairs and grabbed a fleece jacket off the rack by the front door.

I figured I'd walk the couple, three miles east to the lakefront and then treat myself to an Uber to come home. I let Ernie know my plan (he didn't even look up from his iPad) and set off.

In the hallway, though, I stopped.

Paula's door was open and music blared from within. Peggy Lee singing "Is That All There Is?"

I grinned. With all that had gone on, Paula and I had kind of avoided each other. A little time and distance needed to pass, I figured, before we could pick up on making our acquaintance into a proper friendship. I liked Paula a lot and hoped we could make that transition, despite all that had transpired. She made me laugh and the older I got, the more I realized people who could do that were rare and wonderful treasures.

I stuck my head in and was shocked.

Paula didn't see me at first. She was on the floor, legs curled up beneath her, sealing up a box with tape. She wore a ratty gray sweatshirt and faded jeans. Her feet were bare.

Her little studio was filled with similar boxes, all labeled and stacked. The TV was sheathed in bubble wrap. Kitchen cabinet doors hung open and their interiors were empty.

I took a few steps in. "Paula?" My voice echoed a bit.

She jumped a little, startled, and looked up from her work. Wearing no makeup and with her hair tied into a ponytail, she appeared suddenly younger, almost childlike. I noticed for the first time a spray of freckles across the bridge of her nose and upper cheeks. When our eyes met, she gave me what I could interpret as a sheepish grin. Color rose to her face. "Oh, hey," she said, minus her usual sass and bluster. "I didn't hear you sneak in."

I squatted down beside her and asked the obvious, "You're moving?"

She dabbed at a few drops of sweat that had gathered on her forehead with the back of her hand before responding. "How in the hell did you figure that out? What are you, psychic?"

I laughed. "And there's the Paula I know. Seriously, though, you're leaving us, and you didn't think to say anything?" As soon as the words were out of my mouth, I wanted to stuff them back in. They were both entitled and presumptuous. She had no need to inform me, and she had every right to remind me of it.

But she didn't. She got up and her joints cracked. She moaned, rubbing the small of her back. "It sucks getting old. Coffee?"

I knew how much walking I had in store, and coffee would not be my friend—not on a long walk with few restrooms, so I told her I'd love a glass of water.

She ran one for me from the tap. After pouring herself a cup of joe from the press on the counter, she indicated the oak pedestal table near the window.

After shoving aside the boxes stacked on the chairs, we sat.

"Actually, I'm glad you *caught* me. I really needed a break." She took a sip of her coffee, whispered, "Cold. Fuck." She got up to zap it in the microwave.

"I know you didn't need to mention it. It's none of my business."

She sat back down with me and her coffee. "I was gonna stop by and say goodbye to you and Kevin. Really."

"His name's Ernie."

She snorted. "Sorry. Just never really got to know him."

I noticed she didn't add anything about wanting to get to know him.

"So, I have to ask—why the move? I never got the impression you were in the market."

She pondered for a while, a long while, sipping her coffee. And then she came out with a non-sequitur. Or maybe it wasn't. "Karl was arrested last night. It hasn't been on the news or anything far as I know."

"Seriously?" I asked. Paula had been told the lengths he'd gone to ensuring that the call he eventually made to the authorities was totally anonymous. But anonymity is hard to hang on to, I guess.

"Yeah. I don't know all the details, but DNA, fibers or some shit like that, for what I understand, linked him to the body." She took another sip of her coffee and lit a cigarette. She blew the smoke toward the ceiling and sighed. "Not to mention live-in boyfriends are usually the first folks they look at when something like this happens." She shook her head. "He had to know they'd catch up to him. But, I don't know, I feel sorry for Karl, but this feels like justice. You know?"

"What do you think will happen to him?"

Paula shrugged. "Not sure. I'm gonna meet up with Tommy's sister, Amanda, tomorrow for breakfast. I'll know more then. What I do know is that he's already out on bail. From what I would guess, I'd think he's not gonna be on the hook for murder or anything like that." She shook her head. "Whatever happens, it's just a sad footnote to a tragic story."

We fell silent for a bit. An L train rumbled by. And then a car playing rap music with earth-shaking bass rolled by. I can't say for sure which was noisier. The world was carrying on; it slowed for nothing.

"You still haven't told me why you're moving. Evasive, much?" I cocked my head and frowned. "I like having you next door."

She reached across the table and squeezed my hand, then let it go. "You're a sweet kid, you know that? I'll miss you. And who knows? Maybe once I get settled, I'll have you and Bernie over for supper. I make a mean tuna noodle casserole."

"Ernie."

"Right."

Silence claimed the room again and I thought I should go. I can't say why, but I was certain once Paula was out of here, I'd never see her again.

Paula made it easy for me to act on making my departure. "I really need to get back to the drudgery of packing, my dear. Movers are coming in a couple of hours."

I stood. I thought about hugging her, but she didn't seem receptive, staying in her seat at the table. In the end, we were strangers. United by a common thread, now untied.

I moved toward the door.

"Too much bad shit," she said, softly.

I turned.

She gave me a sad smile. "You understand, right?"

I nodded.

"I thought I'd get over losing Tommy the way I did, but when you showed up with your crazy visions and whatnot, it just brought all the hurt back to the surface. I need to shed these memories I have of the boys, move on. A friend of mine from work was looking for a roomie. I'm not big on the idea of grown women living together unless they're in love, but Eleanor's a quiet gal, in sales, and travels a lot. She has a gorgeous old place in a building on Eastlake Terrace, so, from every window, you look out and see the lake. I think I'll find that calming. The lake has many moods."

"It'll be a lot better than these L trains, I'm sure."

"Quieter and prettier."

"In spades." I reached for the doorknob and paused. "Speaking of the lake, I was actually headed out for a long walk beside it. Clear my head."

"Sounds nice. Wish I had that freedom! But duty calls."

I opened the door. "Gotcha. Please leave us your forwarding address. I really would love to stay in touch with you."

Paula at last stood. "Will do, hon. I'll see you around." When she said that, it made me think, oddly, of when I was single and a trick would say he'd "see me around" or words to that effect. The truth was, we never did.

I turned in the open doorway. Because I was worried I might never cross paths with Paula again, I had to ask, "Why do you think this happened to *me*? I mean, why not you? Or Tommy's sister, even? I didn't even know him."

Paula cocked her head. She gazed out the window for a time, then looked back. "Maybe you're a receiver."

I snorted. "You mean like a bottom?" I raised my hand. "Guilty as charged."

Paula chuckled. "Okay. TMI. I just meant that maybe you pick up on stuff most of us don't. I think there's lot of energy hanging around, lots of unseen shit going on most of us are never aware of. Maybe you're different. Maybe it gets through to you. And maybe Tommy was waiting for the right hero to come along to save him from the limbo he was stuck in."

"Oh, I don't know about that." *Me? A hero?*

"I think you know all about that."

And, just like that, I felt seen.

The truth was, I'd had weird stuff happen to me almost my whole life. I shrugged it off, mostly. Put it down to coincidence or an overactive imagination.

But looking back, it was all there, always. Prophetic dreams. Inklings where I just knew when something was about to happen, whether it was good or bad. And most of all, a connection to people on the other side. But I never wanted to acknowledge the latter because it was, well, nuts. And I'd never felt it as strongly as I had with Tommy.

But maybe Tommy needed me the most. I said as much to Paula.

She nodded. "You're a good guy. And you helped him. I really believe that."

I didn't say anything. It was true. I believed it too. But to admit it seemed immodest. "Well, whatever. I should hit the streets, enjoy this beautiful day. They're predicting flurries by Wednesday."

"Don't say that."

"Okay, I won't say that. But maybe, as much as I helped Tommy, he helped me."

"What do you mean?"

I closed the door and leaned on it, debating whether I should share what was on my mind.

"It's Ernie."

"Okay?"

It was weird. I hadn't left the apartment more than fifteen minutes ago, and a big decision was the furthest thing from my mind. But just now, it came to me—sudden and sure.

I needed to end things with Ernie.

He was a wonderful man. Sexy. Warm. Funny.

But I didn't feel a spark with him and now I wondered if I ever had. I thought of him as I left just now, not even looking up from his iPad as I departed. There were no pecks on the cheek, or admonitions to hurry home, or even be careful. Fact was, Ernie was probably as bored with our life together as I was.

I think it wasn't just my own subconscious telling me this, although that was part of it. I think my disillusionment had been swimming around in the deepest murk of my psyche for a long time. Maybe it was why I'd been so drawn to the apartment. Maybe when I signed a lease without asking Ernie, I wanted, in a passive-aggressive way, to escape from him.

But I also think that Tommy, and this whole experience, told me the same. Tommy had been bright, full of potential, in love. And he threw it all away.

Karl didn't kill him. He killed himself.

Drugs were the gun he'd put to his own head.

I wasn't about to let complacency be the gun I put to mine.

Paula stared at me, as though expecting me to say more. But there wasn't really any more to say to her. She didn't even know Ernie's name, and she was moving out to get away from gay men and their relationship woes. So I simply told her, "I have a lot to think about. Fresh air and crashing surf will help."

She nodded, then turned away and began putting boxes in books.

"Take care, Paula."

"Uh-huh."

I left knowing I really didn't have much to think about, beyond how I would tell Ernie the truth. The walk along the lakefront wasn't to sort things out in my head— it was procrastination.

I hurried outside the building.

It was colder than I thought it would be. The blue skies and gilded sun were a lie, as they often were in this town. I wrapped my arms around myself, as a chill wind blew out of the north, making me shiver.

I made another impulsive decision.

The lake would be cold, and its chill would make me miserable.

I thought what I really needed to do was get on an L train and head south. The Music Box theater on Southport would be a great place to escape to. I had no idea what was playing, but it didn't really matter. Sitting in a darkened theater, with the flickering light of the screen pouring over me sounded like a very good idea.

Oblivion...with buttered popcorn.

I smiled and crossed the street, headed up the stairs to the L platform at Irving Park Road.

Because it was a Saturday and I'd just missed a train, I had the platform to myself. The sky, in a short time, had gotten more crowded with clouds, some of them a deep shade of gray. They massed on the eastern horizon and I could imagine how they would have worked their magic on the waters from the lake, transforming it from aquamarine to a foreboding dark.

I shivered.

I don't know where she came from. But all of the sudden, she was there, at the southern end of the tracks. I peered at her because there wasn't much else to look at. She was young, in her teens, what we used to call a Goth chick. She'd apparently missed the memo that the style was now dated and out of favor, for the most part.

She had a short black bob (which I'm sure was the result of dye) and wore a full-length thrift store black wool coat that ended just where her black combat boots began. Her hands were clad in black knit gloves with the fingers cut off. Her nails were predictably lacquered black.

She turned toward me, and I almost stepped off the edge of the platform. Her eyes, dark, were soulless, and they cut straight to my heart. Those eyes were pleading.

I was just thinking of walking toward her to ask if she was okay. Her whole being had a hopeless aspect.

But then I felt more than heard the rumble of an approaching train.

A voice over the loudspeaker squawked. "Attention riders. The next train will not be stopping. It will run express to Fullerton. Fullerton will be the next stop."

I looked to see the train bearing down, blowing its horn, showing no signs of slowing.

I stepped back, anticipating the rush of cold wind the train would leave in its wake.

And then I looked south, to where the young woman was standing. She stood poised on the ledge, toes hanging over the rough wooden boards.

Before I could think, the train roared through into the station.

She jumped.

I screamed, stifling it with my hand.

The train didn't even stop. It continued its rapid passage south.

And when it was gone, there was nothing—and no one—there. But I could hear a small voice in my head, a female voice, saying two words, "Help me."

I walked to the edge of the platform where I had thought I'd seen the Goth chick, thinking maybe there'd be a trace of her.

But of course, there wasn't.

She'd never been there. At least not in this real world.

I moved back and plopped down on a bench, thinking about what Paula had called me. A receiver.

I closed my eyes, shivering against the chill.

The next train couldn't get here soon enough.

About Rick R. Reed

Real Men. True Love.

Rick R. Reed is an award-winning and bestselling author of more than fifty works of published fiction. He is a Lambda Literary Award finalist. *Entertainment Weekly* has described his work as "heartrending and sensitive." *Lambda Literary* has called him: "A writer that doesn't disappoint..." Find him at www.rickrreedreality.blogspot.com. Rick lives in Palm Springs, CA, with his husband, Bruce, and their two rescue dogs, Kodi and Joaquin.

Email
rickrreedbooks@gmail.com

Facebook
www.facebook.com/rickrreedbooks

Twitter
@rickrreed

Website
www.rickrreedreality.blogspot.com

Other NineStar books by this author

Also from NineStar Press

The Man from Milwaukee

It's the summer of 1991 and serial killer Jeffrey Dahmer has been arrested. His monstrous crimes inspire dread around the globe. But not so much for Emory Hughes, a closeted young man in Chicago who sees in the cannibal killer a kindred spirit, someone who fights against the dark side of his own nature, as Emory does. He reaches out to Dahmer in prison via letters.

The letters become an escape—from Emory's mother dying from AIDS, from his uncaring sister, from his dead-end job in downtown Chicago, but most of all, from his own self-hatred.

Dahmer isn't Emory's only lifeline as he begins a tentative relationship with Tyler Kay. He falls for him and, just like Dahmer, wonders how he can get Tyler to stay. Emory's desire for love leads him to confront his own grip on reality. For Tyler, the threat of the mild-mannered Emory seems inconsequential, but not taking the threat seriously is at his own peril.

Can Emory discover the roots of his own madness before it's too late and he finds himself following in the footsteps of the man from Milwaukee?

Excerpt

Dahmer appeared before you in a five o'clock edition, stubbled dumb countenance surrounded by the crispness of a white shirt with pale-blue stripes. His handsome face, multiplied by the presses, swept down upon Chicago and all of America, to the depths of the most out-of-the-way villages, in castles and cabins, revealing to the mirthless bourgeois that their daily lives are grazed by enchanting murderers, cunningly elevated to their sleep, which they will cross by some back stairway that has abetted them by not creaking. Beneath his picture burst the dawn of his crimes: details too horrific to be credible in a novel of horror: tales of cannibalism, sexual perversity, and agonizing death, all bespeaking his secret history and preparing his future glory.

Emory Hughes stared at the picture of Jeffrey Dahmer on the front page of the *Chicago Tribune*, the man in Milwaukee who had confessed to "drugging and strangling his victims, then dismembering them." The picture was grainy, showing a young man who looked timid and tired. Not someone you'd expect to be a serial killer.

Emory took in the details as the L swung around a bend: lank pale hair, looking dirty and as if someone had taken a comb to it just before the photograph was snapped, heavy eyelids, the smirk, as if Dahmer had no understanding of what was happening to him, blinded suddenly by notoriety, the stubble, at least three days old, growing on his face. Emory even noticed the way a small curl topped his shirt's white collar. The L twisted, suddenly a ride from Six Flags, and Emory almost dropped the newspaper, clutching for the metal pole to keep from falling. The train's dizzying pace, taking the curves too fast, made Emory's stomach churn.

Or was it the details of the story that were making the nausea in him grow and blossom? Details like how Dahmer had boiled some of his victim's skulls to preserve them...

Milwaukee Medical Examiner Jeffrey Jentzen said authorities had recovered five full skeletons from Dahmer's apartment and partial remains of six others. They'd discovered four severed heads in his kitchen. Emory read that the killer had also admitted to cannibalism.

"Sick, huh?" Emory jumped at a voice behind him. A pudgy man, face florid with sweat and heat, pressed close. The bulge of the man's stomach nudged against the small of Emory's back.

Emory hugged the newspaper to his chest, wishing there was somewhere else he could go. But the L at rush hour was crowded with commuters, moist from the heat, wearing identical expressions of boredom.

"Hard to believe some of the things that guy did." The man continued, undaunted by Emory's refusal to meet his eyes. "He's a queer. They all want to give the queers special privileges and act like there's nothing wrong with them. And then look what happens." The guy snorted. "Nothing wrong with them...right."

Emory wished the man would move away. The sour odor of the man's sweat mingled with cheap cologne, something like Old Spice.

Hadn't his father worn Old Spice?

Emory gripped the pole until his knuckles whitened, staring down at the newspaper he had found abandoned on a seat at the Belmont stop. *Maybe if he sees I'm reading, he'll shut up.* Every time the man spoke, his accent broad and twangy, his voice nasal, Emory felt like someone was raking a metal-toothed comb across the soft pink surface of his brain.

Neighbors had complained off and on for more than a year about a putrid stench from Dahmer's apartment. He told them his refrigerator was broken and meat in it had spoiled. Others reported hearing hand and power saws buzzing in the apartment at odd hours.

"Yeah, this guy Dahmer... You hear what he did to some of these guys?"

Emory turned at last. He was trembling, and the muscles in his jaw clenched and unclenched. He knew his voice was coming out high, and that because of this, the man might think *he* was queer, but he had to make him stop.

"Listen, sir, I really have no use for your opinions. I ask you now, very sincerely, to let me be so that I might finish reading my newspaper."

The guy sucked in some air. "Yeah, sure," he mumbled.

Emory looked down once more at the picture of Dahmer, trying to delve into the dots that made up the serial killer's eyes. Perhaps somewhere in the dark orbs, he could find evidence of madness. Perhaps the pixels would coalesce to explain the atrocities this bland-looking young man had perpetrated, the pain and suffering he'd caused.

To what end?

"Granville next. Granville will be the next stop." The voice, garbled and cloaked in static, alerted Emory that his stop was coming up.

As the train slowed, Emory let the newspaper, never really his own, slip from his fingers. The train stopped with a lurch, and Emory looked out at the familiar green sign reading Granville. With the back of his hand, he wiped the sweat from his brow and prepared to step off the train.

Then an image assailed him: Dahmer's face, lying on the brown, grimy floor of the L, being trampled.

Emory turned back, bumping into commuters who were trying to get off the train, and stooped to snatch the newspaper up from the gritty floor.

Tenderly, he brushed dirt from Dahmer's picture and stuck the newspaper under his arm.

Kenmore Avenue sagged under the weight of the humidity as Emory trudged home, white cotton shirt sticking to his back, face moist. At the end of the block, a Loyola University building stood sentinel—gray and solid against a wilted sky devoid of color, sucking in July's heat and moisture like a sponge.

Emory fitted his key into the lock of the redbrick high-rise he shared with his mother and sister, Mary Helen. Behind him, a car grumbled by, muffler dragging, transmission moaning. A group of four children, Hispanic complexions darkened even more by the sun, quarreled as one of them held a huge red ball under his arm protectively.

As always, the vestibule smelled of garlic and cooking cabbage, and as always, Emory wondered from which apartment these smells, grown stale over the years he and his family had lived in the building, had originally emanated.

In the mailbox was a booklet of coupons from Jewel, a Commonwealth Edison bill, and a newsletter from *Test Positive Aware*. Emory shoved the mail under his arm and headed up the creaking stairs to the third floor.

*

Mary Helen waited.

A cloud of blue cigarette smoke hung near the ceiling, ethereal. The smoke didn't cover the perfume Mary Helen wore, something called Passion. She had doused so much of it on herself that Emory wanted to cover his nose, to gag, to ask her if she was in her right mind.

But he said nothing, only smiled at his younger sister, who sat, long legs thrown over the arms of a brown corduroy recliner, staring dumbly at the screen. The flickering images of a sitcom made Mary Helen's face alternately light and then dark. Canned laughter erupted every few moments, and Emory prickled. He felt as though they were laughing at *him*.

He cleared his throat, hoping his sister would notice him. There was a time, not so long ago, when he, a fifteen-year-old boy, and she, a little towheaded girl of seven, would sprawl on the living room floor together, newspapers spread out in front of them, and share a box of powdered sugar doughnuts while watching TV together.

Those days were long past. Mary Helen had dropped out of high school in the spring and now seemed to have no occupation other than sitting around the apartment during the day and disappearing to God knows where at night, sometimes not returning until the early morning, when dawn's gray light worked its transformation on the apartment, giving the worn furniture and threadbare carpets definition and color.

"Hello, Mary Helen," Emory moved toward the TV screen. "What are you watching?" A little girl on the television was dramatically rolling her eyes as an older man explained the virtues of telling the truth.

Mary Helen shifted in her seat, put her feet on the floor. She grabbed the remote control from the end table beside her and banished the father and daughter to darkness.

"Nothin'." She lit another cigarette from the butt of the last. She blew a stream of smoke toward her brother.

Emory waved the smoke away. "Have you had anything to eat?"

She glared at him, pursing her lips together. "No. Have you?"

Emory put his briefcase on a spare chair in the dining room, loosened his tie. There was a fan blowing, and Emory stood in front of it. The fan delivered no relief; it merely blew the hot air around more intensely.

"How was Mother today?"

Mary Helen stood and examined a run in the back of her black stockings. "Shit," she whispered to herself, then looked up at her brother. She smiled and her eyes sparkled. For a moment, Emory smiled back, startled to see a return of the cheerful little girl who used to live here.

"Mother had a complete recovery today. In fact, she's not even in her room. She got up around ten, dressed herself in a pink linen dress—charming little chapeau with a veil, stockings, the whole nine yards. She then went down to the L station. Told me she was headed downtown, to fucking Marshall Fields, where she'd do a little shopping and have lunch in the Walnut Room. And then she was going over to Thirty Three Personnel on Dearborn to see if they had anything in her line..." Mary Helen took a deep drag on her cigarette and blew the smoke once more at her brother, shaking her head. "How the fuck do you think she is?"

Emory licked his lips and rubbed his hands together. His palms were sweating.

Mary Helen started toward the door. She wore a black miniskirt and a black leather vest under which was a sheer black-lace body shirt. She had dyed her hair platinum blonde and cut it so that it stood up in hard little spikes. She wore silver hoop earrings, rows of four in descending size, in each ear. Her nose sported a silver stud. Emory wondered what was to be pierced next but could never ask her. She had done her face up to make it paler than it already was and lined her eyes in thick black mascara.

"Did Mother eat anything today?" Emory called after her.

Mary Helen replied by closing the front door softly.

"Does Mother need anything?" he asked the closed door.

Third Eye

Who knew that a summer thunderstorm and a lost little boy would conspire to change single dad Cayce D'Amico's life in an instant? With Luke missing, Cayce ventures into the woods near their house to find his son, only to have lightning strike a tree near him, sending a branch down on his head. When he awakens the next day in the hospital, he discovers he has been blessed or cursed—he isn't sure which—with psychic ability. Along with unfathomable glimpses into the lives of those around him, he's getting visions of a missing teenage girl.

When a second girl disappears soon after the first, Cayce realizes his visions are leading him to their grisly fates. Cayce wants to help, but no one believes him. The police are suspicious. The press wants to exploit him. And the girls' parents have mixed feelings about the young man with the "third eye."

Cayce turns to local reporter Dave Newton and, while searching for clues to the string of disappearances and possible murders, a spark ignites between them. Little do they know that nearby, another couple—dark and murderous—are plotting more crimes and wondering how to silence the man who knows too much about them.

Excerpt

Cayce D'Amico felt the hairs on the back of his neck stand up. The gathering clouds were angry, bruised, hulking blue-gray shapes pressing down on the hills.

"Oh, there's one hell of a storm coming. That's for sure." He watched the darkening sky through the kitchen window, pausing from his work of chopping burdock stalks into sticks for the Sicilian fritters called cardoons. The wind kicked up, audible, becoming icy, the leaves turning to display their pale undersides. The last few days had been the opposite: punishing temperatures in the upper nineties and humidity so thick you could drown in it. Miserable. Cayce had lain in front of a fan in his boxers at night as it whirred and blew the hot air around, offering no relief.

It was like lying inside a convection oven.

He beat eggs, added some grated Romano and salt and pepper, and set the batter next to the burdock stalks. He wiped his hands on a dishtowel.

Worse, though, than the brewing storm outside was the fact he couldn't see his son, Luke. Luke, at seven, was prone to wandering away. Usually such distraction wasn't of much concern, because Fawcettville wasn't like Pittsburgh, about an hour east, with its crime and traffic. Fawcettville perched on the banks of the Ohio River, overlooking the hills of the northern panhandle of West Virginia. It was mostly known as a town where nothing ever happened. Sometimes the inactivity seemed like a drawback, dull. Other times it was a blessing—especially for a single dad bringing up a little boy. Then you appreciated blessings like living in a dull backwater town, where the worst crime you could remember was some kids breaking into Bricker's drug store last summer.

Peace of mind.

So why did Cayce suddenly feel something wasn't quite right? Why did the fact that Luke was no longer in the backyard make him queasy?

Cayce and Luke didn't live in some sort of exclusive area. Their little house was surrounded by others much the same: older houses covered in peeling paint, rusting aluminum siding, or asphalt tile that was supposed to look like brick but never did. Cayce had grown up in this little hollow down by the Ohio River and knew most of his neighbors. Just as they had watched Cayce playing from their porch swings and gliders, many of the same people watched Luke, even though their hair had turned gray and their children had grown up and moved away, especially when the steel mill in a neighboring town had closed down, taking any hope of prosperity with it.

"Maybe it's just the wind making me so cold." Cayce rubbed at the dark hair on his forearms, making the coarse black fur stand on end. He was sure the temperature had dropped at least fifteen degrees in the past half hour. This drop, coupled with the slate-blue clouds perched on the southern horizon, did much to raise the gooseflesh on his forearms. The chill might have been welcome if Luke was at the kitchen table, playing with his Hot Wheels.

But he was not. And Cayce, on the younger side of thirty, knew that at least a portion of the goose bumps on his beefy arms was from a distinct yet inexplicable dread and not the cold breeze, the dark clouds, and the imminent storm making its way into Fawcettville.

The Swiss chard laid out to be cleaned could wait, as could the tomatoes from his garden, still unsliced. Cayce did not like Luke being out where he couldn't see him as weather bore down. He didn't like it at all.

He slid into a pair of flip-flops he kept by the kitchen door. "Oreo!" he called, and a black-and-white mutt about the size of a boxer, with bright brown eyes, bounded into the kitchen, toenails clicking on the linoleum. "Wanna go outside, boy? Wanna help me find Luke?" Oreo had been left behind two years ago by Marc, Cayce's "friend and roommate," as his mother put it. Marc couldn't stand the stifling life of a gay man in a small town and had set out for the bright lights and tall buildings—and easy men—of Pittsburgh. Who knew? Perhaps Marc had been swayed by all the *Queer as Folk* reruns he used to watch. Once he'd packed up his Nissan pickup, Cayce never saw the guy again and had never found love again.

But who the hell had time for that crap!

Cayce didn't know why he ever bothered to think of the man, who had never been much help as a parent to

Luke...or even as a dog owner, for that matter. Marc had been all about Marc. "C'mon, Oreo!"

Outside, the wind was kicking up. Papers and small pieces of gravel skittered across the road in front of the house. Cars passing by had turned on their headlights, piercing the odd, darkening afternoon light. The maple trees lining the road bent in the wind, like fingers splayed backward. The sky had a funny greenish tinge, and Cayce had seen that weird green color enough times to know what the storm portended.

Cayce made his way down First Avenue, searching from side to side and pausing occasionally to rub a piece of grit out of his eye. "Luke!" He yelled, "Luke!" even louder when there was no response. Where was that boy?

A drop of water landed on his arm, icy. The rows of houses lining the yellow-bricked street had deserted porches—everyone escaped indoors. The lights switched on inside the houses made them look like sanctuaries, and Cayce wished he could be in his own sanctuary with his own son, smells of the Sicilian peasant food he had grown up on filling their little house. Cayce supposed his neighbors had all retreated into their living rooms, where they could turn on the Weather Channel or listen to the radio to validate what was happening before their eyes.

Everyone, that was, except for Lula Stewart, bless her. Lula, who had lost her husband the winter before, still sat on her glider, wispy dyed-black hair being lifted by the wind.

"He went thataway," Lula called, pointing to where First Avenue dead-ended at the woods.

"Great," Cayce whispered to himself, then said to Lula, "Thanks. I'm going to wring his little neck for him."

"Be nice, Cayce. He's only seven."

"I know, I know." Cayce headed for the darkness of the trees at the end of the street. As he picked up his pace, so did the wind and the droplets of water, coming heavier every second.

The sky flashed with white light. Cayce gasped as a crack of thunder ripped through the air, reverberating through the ground and leaving in its wake the smell of ozone. "God, that was close." Why didn't Luke have the sense to come in out of the rain?

The sky ripped open and released the downpour, a sibilant hiss, so heavy it nearly blinded Cayce. In seconds his T-shirt and board shorts were drenched, clinging to him like a second skin. Water sluiced from his curly black hair into his eyes. The sky morphed into premature night, brightened only by the lightning. The thunder's crash upped Cayce's sense of anxiety and fear with each crack. The volume and the bright lightning seemed to have a direct line to his heart, which hammered double time in his chest.

"Luke!" he screamed above the wind that yanked twigs and whole clumps of leaves from the trees above him. An orange drink carton hit Cayce in the back of the head.

"Luke!" He watched in despair as Oreo ran back toward the house, tail between his legs. "Traitor," he called after the dog.

The woods were even darker than the street. Cayce held his hands out in front of him to avoid crashing into trees. Already, his flip-flops were making a sucking sound as he pulled his feet out of the mud.

Annoyed, Cayce wiped the icy rain away from his face, flinging his damp mop of black hair back, trying to see in the storm's murk. In the brief bluish flash of lightning, the woods looked empty, deserted. Why couldn't he see Luke cowering under a tree, or better yet, running toward him, hell, even running *away* from him? Anything but this dreadful emptiness, abandoning him to the woods and the storm.

"Luke!" he yelled again, his throat growing hoarse. He tried to keep his voice even so Luke wouldn't think he was mad, so the little boy wouldn't hear his dad's fear. "Luke, if you can hear me, yell. I'm not mad."

And he wasn't, not at his little boy anyway, whom he pictured trembling under a tree or huddled under a neighbor's porch, shivering, terrified, wet, and cold. But Cayce *was* angry at himself, for not keeping better tabs on the weather and the whereabouts of a seven-year-old. What was wrong with him? Maybe his mom was right; maybe Cayce was too young (and alone) to take on the responsibility of rearing another human being. She was always telling Cayce to give the boy back to his mother. "Little boys need their moms," his own mom often proclaimed.

Apparently, though, moms didn't always need their little boys. Case in point, Joyce, Cayce's wife of less than a year, who was only too happy to leave the "burden" of Luke with Cayce when she abandoned them both four years ago, heading off without a backward glance for the presumably greener pastures of Portland, Oregon. Like Marc, Joyce apparently believed happiness awaited *outside* the city limits of Fawcettville, Pennsylvania.

"Luke!" he called once more, competing for dominance with the wind, the thunder, the driving rain.

But all that answered him was the roar of the storm and the sound of detritus whistling through the air and smacking against the trees. Cayce was beginning to think his quest was in vain, that Luke was probably already at home, sitting at the kitchen table and wondering where his dad was, hungry for his supper.

It happened so quickly Cayce only experienced the event through instincts, like an animal.

The flash was so bright, Cayce gasped, squeezing his eyes shut.

The scent of ozone filled the air. Hair stood up on the back of his neck, tickling.

The rumble of the thunder deafened, so loud and close it drowned out his scream. And the sharp break of the tree branch above his head was akin to the crack of a whip.

The limb crashing down on his head dropped him to his knees. Everything went dark.

Connect with NineStar Press

www.ninestarpress.com

www.facebook.com/ninestarpress

www.facebook.com/groups/NineStarNiche

www.twitter.com/ninestarpress

www.instagram.com/ninestarpress